Beyond Blaming

Unleashing Power and Passion in People and Organizations

William Frank Diedrich

Beyond Blaming

Unleashing Power and Passion in People and Organizations

William Frank Diedrich

www.noblaming.com

What people have said about **Beyond Blaming**

A very popular error: "I'm right; others are wrong." Bill Diedrich's compelling book clearly exposes this thought trap, and the negative consequences that it has for individuals and organizations. He shows us a path that leads us far away from this mental maze. The book is full of practical and inspiring insights and effective suggestions on how to free ourselves from the blaming trap. If you have the courage to examine your convictions about the offenses that others have supposedly inflicted upon you, then read this book, and learn how to disengage from these energy sapping thoughts. **Beyond Blaming** is a powerful vision that leads individuals and organizations into responsive, caring and uplifting relationships.

Herb Bursch
President and CEO
First National Bank of Howell, Michigan

Beyond Blaming presents important advice and opportunities for growth for an organization. Author Bill Diedrich captures and identifies examples of unproductive and counterproductive applications of human and organizational energies, talent, time, and resources too frequently devoted to blame as opposed to corrective and growth opportunities. Every organization would profit by addressing every issue for its future potential, even if in limiting future missteps, rather than documenting and promoting perceived trails of fault. **Beyond Blaming** carries an important message.

Dennis Koons, CAE, JD,
President and CEO
Michigan Bankers Association

Beyond Blaming is an excellent guide for a common issue at work and home. Learning how to both stop yourself from blaming and respond to others' blaming begins with the first page!

Stephen White,
Advisory Quality Engineer

If you want to move from a mindset of blaming to a mindset of balance, **Beyond Blaming** by Bill Diedrich is the only book you will ever need to read on the subject.

Philippe Matthews
(Publisher: SHOCKphilosophy.com)

Once again, William Diedrich, in his insightful book **Beyond Blaming** addresses complex issues with courage and integrity. He outlines simple yet effective strategies to resolve inner conflict, create rich relationships and manage the paradoxes of power. In effect he opens a kaleidoscope of possibilities enabling the reader to create a more successful personal andprofessional life."

Dolores Cummins,
CEO, Lifelink International

A profound and timely book. **Beyond Blaming** will make a dramatic difference for those serious about increasing personal power and inspiring extraordinary performance in others.

Tess Marshall,
Author of Flying by the Seat of My Soul

William Diedrich's writing is "radical" in that takes one directly to the root of an issue. He teaches us the proper sequence of problem solving by leading us inward with clarity and integrity. Bill lives what he teaches, and he is a favorite speaker and workshop presenter among our congregation. I frequently hear good reports from those who have taken his internet courses about how their lives have been positively changed."

Reverend Barbara Jung,
Unity Church of Peace

Beyond Blaming
Unleashing Power and Passion in People and Organizations

Book design by Joshua Diedrich
Cover illustration copyright Joshua Diedrich 2004

Revised Edition

ISBN 0-9710568-6-2

10 9 8 7 6 5 4 3 2 1

Printed in the USA

Also by William Frank Diedrich and Transformative Press:
The Road Home, the Journey Beyond the Spiritual Quick Fix
30 Days to Prosperity: A Workbook for Well-Being

Transformative Press
East Lansing, Michigan
www.transformativepress.com

Beyond Blaming
www.noblaming.com

There is no blame

To my father

Beyond Blaming

Unleashing Power and Passion in People and Organizations

Contents

Introduction

Do you want peace? Do you feel truly successful in your work, your relationships, your finances, and in your health? Are your workplace, your family, and your community working well? You have the power to create peace instead of excessive stress and conflict. You have the ability to help yourself and others to be successful. To accomplish all of this you have to give up one thing. This one thing is painful, causes misery and suffering, drives people to violence, and prevents you from achieving your goals. You would think this would be reason enough to give it up. You would think most of us would be letting go of this thing in an instant.

This one thing that makes us suffer is also something we fight to keep. We identify with it. We invest our well being in it. We remind ourselves about it over and over again so that we won't forget it. It disempowers us. It distorts our ability to see reality. This one thing that we need to give up is blaming. Without blaming we are 100% responsible. 100% responsible means that we are completely able to respond to any situation. If we are able to respond we have power.

I wrote this book because I am an expert on blaming. I have done it all my life. I have blamed spouses, children, parents, friends, neighbors, coworkers, the government, the economy, other nations, TV, poor people, rich people, and myself. You name it and I've blamed it. One day I discovered the common denominator. In every relationship, whether personal or professional, where there was strain, irritation, or conflict, there has been one common denominator.

I was there.

The value of this discovery is that it gives me leverage. Instead of spending my energy resisting people and things that are outside of my control, I can focus my attention on the only thing I can control—my thoughts. It is the understanding that I am the common denominator that has led me to adopt the daily practice of moving beyond blaming.

What happens when you choose to move beyond blaming? Power is unleashed within you. Success comes more easily. Your passion is sparked and it drives you in a positive direction. You become disinterested in negativity, complaining, and judging. You become very interested in creating your vision, living it, and manifesting it. Your focus is sharpened. Your commitment is strengthened. Your impact on other people is positive. You become an inspiration to others.

The choice is clear. On one side you have suffering, pain, unresolved conflict, stifled goals, frustration, victimization, and the ability to tell yourself you are the one who is right. On the other side you have peace, happiness, success, goal attainment, empowerment, positive relationships, and the ability to do the right things. Which do you choose?

If the idea of having peace, success, and happiness is attractive to you, read this book. If the idea of creating families, organizations, and relationships that achieve a high level of success is attractive, read this book. If you prefer to hold on to suffering and frustration, insist on being right in your conflicts, and find it attractive to be a victim, then this book could be a threat to your viewpoint. Read it at your own risk. Either way, reading this book will change the way you look at life. It may even motivate you to move beyond blaming and spark the passion and power that is already within you. It may motivate you to become the kind of leader who can spark the passion and power of your organization, your family, a relationship, or the world.

Your possibilities await.

The thought manifests as the word. The word manifests as the deed.

The deed develops into habit and habit hardens into character. So watch the thought and its ways with care, and let it spring from love, born out of concern for all beings. As the shadow follows the body, as we think, so we become.

The Buddha

1 Why We Blame

My first career was as a teacher. Despite the fact that I struggled through numerous mistakes in my first year, my manager (the school principal), a man named Ted Center, never blamed me for anything. He met with me frequently, asked me how I was doing, encouraged me, and offered helpful suggestions. He told me that he saw me struggling at times, but that he knew I was working at it. He had confidence in me. As a result, I not only made it through that year, but I became confident and competent for my second year.

Ted gave me a foundation that served me well in later positions, both in education and in the business world, where criticism and blame were often the norm. Certainly people who have blamed me have helped me to grow stronger, but people like Ted have inspired and empowered me. Ted was powerful because he helped me to become more powerful. He believed in me during a time when I couldn't offer much evidence as to my effectiveness. He offered me his blessing rather than his blaming and that made the difference for me, and for all of the lives that I have touched since.

If you are like most people, you probably don't like being blamed for anything. Blame is the gift almost everyone wants to give, yet no one wants to receive. Blame's message is a very simple and appealing one: there is a reason behind your suffering, and that reason is probably beyond your control. The purpose of blaming is the establishment of guilt. To lay blame is to conclude that a person, thing, or situation is the cause of something painful, of something failed or gone wrong. Despite appearances, laying blame does not help us understand or solve problems, or remedy pain. Its only accomplishments are condemnation, criticism, and the assignment of fault.

Blaming seems like the normal thing to do when things go wrong. Laying blame establishes who the heroes and villains of a situation are, plotting out a story in our minds that can be very satisfying to tell ourselves. Once we have our story, all of the guilt, as well as the power to change our situation, is placed outside of us. Even when we blame ourselves, we put ourselves in a place of no control. Blaming is so satisfying precisely because it makes us *feel* like we are doing something, even if all we are doing is wallowing in guilt. Blaming does nothing to solve a problem. It is, in fact, a substitute for action. It only tells us who should receive our negative thoughts and emotion, not how to resolve problems with them. It often makes problems worse by telling us we can't really do anything to affect the situation. It renders us powerless, but offers us an illusion of having power.

Blaming is a futile attempt to make our world right. Often, it appears to work in the short term, but there are long-term ramifications. As we become more successful at repeatedly pinning the blame on others, our list of enemies grows longer. When a leader in any organization blames employees, clients, members, or customers, blaming becomes an accepted way to deal with problems in that organization. It creates an environment of fear where people are unlikely to take responsibility for problems. In the end, few problems are solved and performance is stifled. People who constantly blame lose the respect of others. Why is it then, that blaming is so common?

Blaming creates several payoffs:

Payoff 1. It can be wonderful to be a victim. I get to be right. I'm misunderstood, mistreated, and miserable, but at least I know I'm right. I'm in pain, but my pain is at least a little bit satisfying. The end all and be all for most of us when we are in the victim mode is self-righteousness — being the one who is right, good, or special. I feel a little bit powerful riding on the back end of the pointing finger. I feel clean and in the clear knowing that it's not my fault.

Payoff 2. If I'm really suffering you can't expect much from me. As the suffering one, I should be appreciated, treated as special, or helped. You can't expect me to put out too much energy for others in this condition. You can't expect me to do much for myself. Again, I'm in the clear.

Payoff 3. It feeds my need for drama. Most dramas have their good guys and bad guys. Of course, I'm usually the good guy in mine. I can tell my story with passion about how I have suffered and how you have caused it. I enjoy telling myself and others how stupid, bad, evil, idiotic, foolish, inconsiderate, lazy, or incompetent you have been. In my drama, I get to be the judge of right and wrong.

Payoff 4. Blaming means that my shortcomings are not my fault. All the bad things that have happened to me or that have been done to me are the reason I am in this state. My negative behaviors, critical thoughts, or lack of progress are justifiable because of what was done to me. I justify myself by adding up the faults of others, and adding up all the reasons why I am right, justified, or innocent.

Payoff 5. Blaming allows me to avoid looking at myself. I tell myself the problem is outside of me. My focus becomes preserving my image of myself as a good parent, good manager, good spouse, or moral person. To look at myself honestly is a threat to one of my most prized possessions - my image of myself.

In the world today, blaming often takes the form of self-righteous indignation. Righteous anger is energy. This energy feels better than the energy of feeling insulted, picked on, taken advantage of, or hurt. Anger feels powerful. Extreme self-righteous anger seems to justify verbal attack, revenge, selfish pursuit of one's own agenda, and violence. In a state of righteous anger we give ourselves permission to say and do things we would ordinarily see as wrong.

These actions make us feel as if we are no longer victims. We feel as if we are taking charge.

When victimhood becomes self-righteous indignation, the emotional payoff we receive is the feeling of power and the idea that we can overcome the enemy. This is not real power that we feel, however; it is the use of force. Dr. David Hawkins writes in his book, *Power Vs. Force*, "Force always creates counterforce; its effect is to polarize rather than unify. Polarization always implies conflict; its cost, therefore, is always high. Because force incites polarization, it inevitably produces a win-lose dichotomy; and because somebody always loses, enemies are created. Constantly faced with enemies, force requires constant defense." Defensiveness is always costly whether in personal relationships, in organizations, in politics, or in international affairs. Defensiveness weakens you, because you constantly need to justify yourself. Your energy is spent on defensive maneuvers rather than on achieving your goals.

True power requires a deeper meaning, something beyond the desire to win or dominate. An idea can be powerful. If people in another department at work are giving my department poor service, I can demand good service. I can use my self-righteous anger to complain and push for what I think is right. I can force them to improve service. I may get what I want, on some level, but the other department will resent me for it. It is unlikely they will really be giving me their best service. They will merely be doing the minimum they can to avoid my wrath. True power requires that I stop blaming. Real power doesn't lie in what I can make people do, but in my vision that the two departments can work together cooperatively for our mutual benefit. If people were excited by that vision, I wouldn't have to *make* them do anything. Both departments would thrive, and as a result, the whole company would prosper.

Rather than putting our energy into looking for opportunities to be offended, why not focus our energy on the peace, prosperity, and joy we want to create? Energy focused on these matters is uplifting. It creates hope, and a passion for the possible.

Ask yourself this question: what is it that makes the United States truly powerful? Is it military might? Or, is it the idea of freedom and democracy for everyone? Think about this. There have been many nations with strong armies throughout history. Did people around the world dream of a new life in Soviet Russia because its military strength would keep them safe from invasion? Of course not. Safety is not enough. People want to prosper and pursue happiness. Take this principle and apply it to your own life. What would make you most powerful at work? Would it be blaming, complaining, and manipulating others? Or, would it be holding and living a vision of excellence for the organization and high respect for others? Which course would bring you influence and the trust of others? Which course do you think would most likely help you to accomplish your goals? Which course would open you up to new possibilities?

There is no argument here regarding the need for a military. In the world's present state of consciousness, force often seems necessary to resist aggressive attacks. The point is, much of the world fears the USA for its military might. Much of the world also respects and admires the USA for its freedom and democracy. If the USA is seen as the world bully, the "bully" will constantly have to defend itself. If the world sees the USA as a beacon of freedom and democracy, as a shining example of peace and prosperity, the shining example will serve as an admired teacher and friend.

Again, apply this thought to your own work situation. Are you the intimidating force who must constantly defend your interests, or are you the admired teacher and friend who helps others feel empowered? Which one do you think has more power?

We are so caught up in the payoffs of blaming that we lose sight of that which would make us successful. Blaming leads us down a dead end street where there are no possibilities, only justifications. Through blaming we are constantly creating resistance to our goals and desires. Through blaming we are maintaining and reinforcing problems rather than solving them.

Problems are always opportunities for greatness. They are the doorways through which we must walk to find success. The choice to succeed is always ours. We can choose to be a victim, make others out to be enemies, and invest in the drama. The alternative is to choose to shake free of blaming and soar to the heights of possibility. Possibility thinking is the ability to see a positive potential in any situation. A possibility thinker moves beyond blaming into the realm of potential success by refusing to blame, refusing to be a victim, and claiming responsibility.

This is the choice you make each and every waking moment of your day. With each thought you are either moving forward into greater possibilities, or you are disempowering yourself with blaming.

Try this little experiment. Pick a day when things are not going especially well. Monitor your thoughts for two hours. Use a notepad and check in with yourself every ten minutes. Ask yourself if you:

- criticized or complained about another person or group of people;
- criticized or complained about an event or situation;
- criticized or complained about something you did or didn't do;
- became upset or irritated because someone else didn't do something;
- became upset or irritated because someone did something you didn't like;
- thought something was unfair.

Use tick marks to record the number of thoughts that fell into these categories. If you spent ten minutes building a case against someone, that counts as more than one thought. Each "reason" you thought about, each piece of "evidence" you pondered, and each criticism are separate thoughts to be counted. You may have to estimate. How many times in two hours did you entertain critical or blaming thoughts? How often did you find yourself midstream in a continuous flow of critical thoughts toward someone?

We are all in this together. If you thought negatively fifty times in the last two hours I can't blame you. It doesn't help me to blame you. It disables us both. I want to help you and myself spend less time blaming and gain greater power in our lives. Blaming ourselves will not improve things.

Each time we blame we abdicate our power to whoever or whatever we are blaming. If you spend your day blaming and complaining, you are letting your power leak away, draining your ability to create success, and focusing your energy on what you don't want.

Blaming is not wrong or bad. We do it because we think it works. Initially we appear to feel better. We blame a person or situation and there is a little relief. "It's not me." We avoid the guilt. The assignment of guilt to another makes us feel a little better about ourselves. Blaming is a distortion of reality. In blaming we deceive ourselves into imagining causes are outside of us. It's the other person, the government, the economy, or the media. Blaming is an illusion that keeps us out of touch with reality. In the real world there is no blame, because there is no "outside".

As human beings we are not objective observers *of* our lives but active participants *in* our lives. As an active participant, you and the cause of your problems are ingredients in the same recipe. To see yourself as separate from cause, to be a complete victim, is a distortion.

This distortion has us seeing ourselves as innocent and others as guilty. It has us deceiving ourselves that someone or something else has a problem. It teaches us that power comes from manipulating externals. Our self-deception has us ignoring the fact that we are helping to create and maintain the current state; that we are creating and maintaining our relationships; and that our unique way of seeing the world is creating the way we feel.

Even when we know that blaming distorts reality, it is unlikely we can completely transcend the need to blame. As emotional human beings we tend to be reactive. We can become aware of it. We can learn to control and release blame. We can transform our perceptions that have us blaming into new, more empowering perceptions. We can transform the person we are being when we are blaming to a new and greater possible human. You will learn how to do that in this book.

It isn't easy to look within and acknowledge the part we have played in creating problems. It isn't easy to stop deceiving ourselves by blaming others. It isn't easy to let go of our attachment to being right and see the truth. It may not be easy, but ultimately it is easier to live with accountability and responsibility than with self-deception and blaming. The misery created through self-deception and blaming is far worse than the discomfort found in accountability and responsibility. If blaming leads us into a dead end, then responsibility leads us out of the mess and into the realm of possibility. Blaming is unending discomfort and victimhood. Taking responsibility is temporary discomfort that turns to victory.

To be blameless is to keep our power rather than giving it away. To be powerful is to be effective. With blame out of the way, our path to success is open. We can be the powerful beings we are meant to be. Our organizations can become focused, engaged, highly competent groups that enjoy peak performance. The question is: Are you interested and willing to be more powerful? Are you willing to move out of the neighborhood of victimhood and into the tower of power? If you are, then you are invited on a journey to greatness — a journey beyond blaming.

Summary: We blame because there are payoffs in being a victim. These payoffs get in the way of our success. Self-righteous anger makes us feel powerful, but does little to solve problems or help us succeed. Real power comes not from blaming what is, but from envisioning what can be.

2 The Problem With Blaming

All human beings suffer, and some suffer more than others. All of us can point to specific people or situations that led to our suffering. Other people often behave cruelly or selfishly and cause pain. Situations can be stressful, painful, or seemingly unworkable. The conditions in our lives can be miserable. It isn't hard to prove that someone did something that led to our suffering. The point of this book is that blaming the seeming source of our pain doesn't make anything better. Blaming is a substitute for real understanding and action, and it usually makes the suffering worse. Like overusing a credit card, whatever short-term rush and benefit you might get is soon far outweighed by the new problem.

What is the problem created by blaming? Blaming costs time and money in organizations. It makes governments ineffective. It creates suffering in relationships. Marriages end because couples blame each other. Fathers and sons refuse to talk to one another; mothers and daughters can't talk without arguing; and siblings avoid each other. Blaming prevents people from seeing solutions to their problems. Blaming can lead to violence, destruction, and death. Blaming, itself, is a problem.

In our modern world, blaming is a way of life. On the international stage leaders of nations blame each other. Terrorists blame those that they terrorize. The justification for the destruction of the World Trade Center and the deaths of thousands of people was blame. Those who were aligned with the terrorists felt the United States got what it deserved. When American troops invaded Afghanistan and Iraq, many Americans believed the Taliban and Saddam Hussein got what they deserved.

In blaming, the people who are blamed become objects. They are not real people. When people become objects we cease to attach any importance to what they want or need. As objects, they are in the way. It is very difficult to shoot or drop bombs on real people. It is unlikely the terrorists who leveled the World Trade Center thought about the needs and concerns of the people who would be killed.

In the War on Terror we blame the terrorists and seek to eliminate them, but force creates counterforce. The War on Terror creates more terrorists. This is not to say people shouldn't be brought to justice. The problem with the blaming approach is that we don't ask some important questions. Why did they do it? Why do so many young men want to join their ranks? What are their needs and concerns regarding their lives? What impact are American policies, American military presence, and American companies having on peoples in other countries? How do people experience *America* in other countries? Can we really expect to eliminate terrorism without understanding the hearts and minds of those who support it? What are their needs and can we help them get their needs met in a peaceful way?

Antiwar groups blame governments for their military activity. This kind of blaming is no more effective than any other. A story about Mother Teresa says she was asked to participate in an antiwar march during the Viet Nam War. She replied: "No, I won't, but if you have a march for peace, I'll be there." Fighting against war is another kind of war. The war makers become the enemy — another object to be blamed. Blaming blocks our vision. It makes us unable to see ourselves or others clearly. Blaming says that someone else's needs are less important, less worthy, and of less value.

Blaming ignores the fact that we share this life (this workplace, this family, this relationship, this nation, this world) with other people, and that it is in our best interests that we be concerned for them. When we blame situations or events, we resist their reality. Trapped in our resistance and anger about the effects of the event, we are blind to the causes, and to the solutions to our problems. We assume that if we deny that those who have hurt us are people like ourselves, if we direct enough rage and resistance at them, they will eventually just go away. What we resist will persist. Other people's wants or needs will not cease to be important or vital to them simply because we wish they would. The harder we push on others, the harder they will push back. Blaming has us focused on forcing the outside world to be different. In blaming, we forget about our best interests, and focus on our fears.

Two women in the same workplace are convinced each other is a bad person. Gena claims Cindy is careless and doesn't do her job. Cindy claims Gena is critical and bossy. Mutual blame prevents them from working together. Their continuous conflict negatively affects other employees, hurts productivity, uses their manager's time, and creates a reputation for their department. Both women say they want a peaceful, productive, and positive workplace. Both claim that it is the other person who prevents that from happening.

They see each other as "the enemy," but where is the real enemy? It is within themselves. Neither can see how their blaming affects the other. Both feel completely justified in treating each other with disrespect. They have a strong emotional reaction to each other's behaviors. They consistently assume the worst about each other. As long as they are caught up in the blame game they cannot see each other.

Whether we are talking about wars between nations, groups, or individuals, blaming takes over our emotions. Unless we become willing to self-reflect, to acknowledge the insanity of blaming, we are stuck in conflict. Our judgments may be somewhat accurate. Cindy may be a little forgetful and scattered; Gena may be domineering and hard to talk to. They may also each bring larger talents to the table that outweigh those flaws. What makes them both more of a problem to others than an asset is their dislike for each other's annoyances, and their mutual inability to see the deeper human being. The blaming and resistance are the real problem.

Many years ago I was a public school teacher. My middle school students were very talkative, more so than I thought appropriate. I told them to be quiet. They would become quiet and then gradually resume talking, increasing their volume to previous levels. I would become frustrated, increase my volume, and tell them to be quiet. I found both our volumes to be increasing each day. I was expending a great deal of effort at noise management. I blamed the students. "What is the matter with them?" I asked." I go to all this effort to provide interesting lessons and still they make too much noise."

In blaming the students I had only one option, the use of force. Increasing my volume, punitive measures, and stricter rules were my means. As the problem continued, I found that I was angry and at war with my students. I decided that what I was doing wasn't working. My force would always create counterforce. If I were successful in forcing them to be quiet, there would be fear, resentment, and resistance to learning on their part. I recognized the contradiction in my efforts. I was yelling at them to be quiet. Worse, I saw their noise as a negative reflection of my skill as a teacher. My image as a teacher was being threatened. I decided to stop *pushing* for what I wanted and to start *being* what I wanted.

The next day I conducted my classes in silence. I used written words and gestures to communicate. The students became quiet. They were waiting for me to speak. They were concerned and a little confused that I wasn't speaking. What I had tried in vain to accomplish through blaming and yelling was easily accomplished through silence. The following day I spoke in a firm, quiet voice. I communicated my expectations. I asked them for their expectations, and what kind of class they wanted. I stopped worrying about whether or not I was a skilled teacher and began just using my skills. My success came only after I was willing to give up blaming. My success came after I stopped trying to force them to be quiet. Instead I put into action my vision for a quieter and more pleasing classroom. I became my vision and that was powerful.

Summary: The problem with blaming is that it usually makes situations worse, not better. Blaming is not a solution; it is, itself, a problem. Our resistance to a person or situation increases its power over us. Blaming and the use of force creates more resistance.

3 The Cost of Blaming

Blaming costs us in time, money, and lost opportunities. You have only to observe the "typical" organization in order to see this. An executive is paid over $100,000 per year and he is known as a strong manager with excellent relationships with his staff. He has several year's worth of e-mails stored, and he knows where every one of them is located. The purpose for keeping and cataloging these thousands of e-mails is protection. They are available in case he needs to prove he is not wrong. How much time does this $100,000 plus executive spend storing e-mails and documenting his actions? How much has this activity taken away from his productivity and his personal time? If he is part of a large company where most of the executives are keeping their e-mails, what is the cost to the organization in time and lost productivity?

Fear of being blamed causes people to invest their time in self-protective strategies rather than productive work. People fear blame so much they cover up mistakes, shift the blame, and invest time and energy into doing whatever is necessary to avoid blame.

Few people have any idea of the cost of their tendency to blame. I have often coached leaders who were seen as bad managers. In one case in particular, several employees constantly complained about their manager's disposition. They complained to each other, to people in other departments, and to whoever would listen. I was asked to come in and work with the manager.

We used a survey to assess attitudes and observations about the manager. We found that several people consistently had a negative view of the manager regarding communications, relationships, and tendency to blame. It became obvious that the manager's way of being with his employees was creating stress and conflict. The manager and I discussed the issues and created a plan for coaching and improvement.

This manager's way of being with his employees was not the only problem. They blamed him for what they saw as his attitude and behavior. Their blaming was also a problem. It served to create a negative image of their department throughout the organization. This negative perception of him was passed on to others who had never met him. Expecting problems, people approached him with defensiveness, and in some cases, with aggression.

Blaming the manager became an easy excuse for not being respectful, not getting the work done on time, and for mistakes. When we blame in organizations, we need to ask: "What impact does our blaming have on this organization?" If I blame another department for being slow to respond, how does that affect the way I do business with them? I might complain about them to others. I might make jokes about them to others. I might approach them with an attitude that is less than professional. I might go around them. My belief in their "slowness" might have me not asking them for much needed help.

Leaders are often targets for blame. While it is true that they are responsible, the blaming hides a multitude of issues. Years ago, I worked out of the corporate office for an entrepreneur who owned several companies. One company had a very autocratic leader who was not well liked by his senior executives. I received a call for help one day from one of the executives. Our chief operating officer (my manager) and I went to visit the company. He spoke with the CEO of the company while I had conversations with individual senior managers. At the conclusion of our meetings the CEO became angry, threw his keys on the desk, and walked out. He was upset with me because he believed I was instigating something with his managers. Of course, this wasn't true. Despite his autocratic ways, I liked the guy. The senior managers were ecstatic that he had left.

Within a few months we hired a new CEO who had high expectations, and he knew how to handle people. The company was in trouble and he needed strong leaders on his team. Within a few months of his hiring, all of the senior managers were let go for various performance issues. Previously they could blame the CEO for their inability to perform. When the previous CEO walked out the door, so did their excuses. All of them had been "yes" men for the previous CEO. Often autocrats surround themselves with people who are afraid to challenge them. The CEO blamed his people for mistakes. They blamed him behind his back. In the meantime, the company had been slowly dying.

Blaming can be an especially costly practice for the people in leadership positions. I have found many managers who blame customers and other managers in front of their own employees. This causes several problems. First, it costs you your credibility as a leader. Your blaming and complaining tells your employees that you are powerless, a victim. They lose respect for you. Second, you teach your employees that it's okay to blame and complain about customers and other employees. Blaming customers sets up a negative attitude toward them. Third, this affects service. As customers, none of us likes being treated with disrespect. Fourth, blaming and complaining set up a negative environment. This is both draining and unpleasant for everyone. If you have ever worked with someone who blames and complains all day, you know what a draining experience that can be.

Blaming prevents us from solving problems. True causes to problems remain hidden because people are afraid to take ownership. A manufacturing company was losing business due to late shipments of their products. At a manager's meeting the manufacturing manager was asked about the problem. He was defensive and blamed the other managers for not helping. The other managers asked him what he needed from them. He was unable to be specific. The CEO formed a committee to study the problem.

The manufacturing manager was afraid to admit that he didn't know what to do. He felt powerless and blamed his colleagues. Their offer of help was an opportunity for him to be powerful. Having the answers is powerful. Facilitating a team of problem solvers is more powerful. Being willing to listen to their ideas and their feedback is powerful. To be willing to say: "I am 100% responsible for this problem, and I could use your help in solving it" is powerful. Asking for help is a response. In his attempt to avoid losing face he lost the respect of his colleagues and gave away his power.

The CEO was unwilling to hold him accountable. Time ran out for this company. The situation worsened until they eventually went out of business. Fear of being blamed or embarrassed prevents us from effectively analyzing risk. Thinking isn't clear. When people in leadership accept blaming instead of expecting responsibility they put their whole organization at risk.

Summary: The cost of blaming is in the blaming itself. Blaming uses up time, money and energy.

4 Kick Your But's

Blaming is not always obvious. It is both subtle and pervasive in the ways that we act and speak. Using the conjunction "but" is often a sign of blaming. Most intelligent people are willing to say: "I am responsible. I am accountable." To say and mean this is the first step. The second step is to add the word "completely". "I am completely responsible." This is difficult for most. When something goes wrong we tend to say: "I am responsible but..." Our *but's* get in the way of assuming complete responsibility. Complete responsibility increases your ability to accomplish goals. Complete responsibility is power. In order to assume complete responsibility we have to kick our *but's*.

But is another way of shifting responsibility. We express good intentions and then negate them with *but*. Examples are:

"I want to work well with that employee, but he's a jerk."

"I want to start my business, but my spouse won't support it."

"I want to help these people, but they are unreasonable."

"I'd like to be more honest, but she won't listen."

"I'd like to do a high quality job, but management keeps getting in my way."

"I'd get this done on time, but I have too much work to do."

But is the great negator. Whatever words you say in the first part of the sentence are erased by the word *but*. When someone says: "I really want to make this work, but these people won't cooperate" — *but* negates "really wanting to make this work." "Those people won't cooperate" is the main message. You may as well say it's over and it's not going to happen. You have convinced yourself that the reason it isn't happening is them. You are abdicating responsibility to them by inferring that they should change.

When we externalize reasons for something not working, we deceive ourselves. Our deception is that it's all them. What impact do I have on this situation? How do I come across to *them*? Have I considered their needs, concerns, and desires? How might I see them and this situation differently?

I become completely responsible when I kick my *but*. I change *but* to *and* and *won't cooperate* to *aren't buying into my plan at this moment*. Now I say: "I really want to make this work, and those people aren't buying into my plan at this moment." Instead of condemning others for not agreeing with me, I can be listening to their concerns and reasons. I can become willing to hear another perspective, and to address their concerns. I can become willing to make adjustments based on new data I may not have been aware of previously. Taking into consideration their needs and concerns, I can present a plan, an adjusted plan, or a new plan to them. Having been heard by me, they are now more willing to listen.

To be completely responsible means that I have the ability to respond to the people and the situation. Responding effectively means caring, listening, and taking effective action. In responding I see the needs and concerns of others as valid for them. It is not an issue whether or not I agree with their needs and concerns. It is not an issue whether or not I think they should have those needs and concerns. I cannot influence others from a place of disconnection. I must connect with them by hearing them, caring about them, and understanding them. I may or may not be able to give them what they want. Giving people what they want is always secondary. Giving them what they need is primary. People need to be heard, to be respected, to be treated as important, and to be given honest, straight forward information.

Anger and frustration with the other people is a sign that I am not taking full responsibility. I am sitting on my *but.* I am blaming them for my inability to move forward. As long as I am sitting on my *but*, I have only two options:

1. Continue to struggle and make little or no progress.

2. Use force to get what I want. (This may include punitive action, threat, intimidation, manipulation, or violence.)

As we know, force always creates counterforce. There will be consequences. You may feel victorious if others are doing what you think is the right thing to do. The real victory is when they are doing the right thing because <u>they</u> choose to do it. This is influence. This is leadership. This is power through complete responsibility.

The principle of complete responsibility also works in dealing with larger situations. Example: "We have a great service to offer, but a slow economy is costing us sales."

Instead of limiting ourselves by blaming our decrease in sales on the economy, why not think in terms of possibilities. Why don't we get off our collective *but* and look for new, previously not thought of ways to offer our services?

Kicking our *buts* causes us to be more thoughtful, more creative, and more powerful. To say and mean, regardless of the situation, "I am completely responsible" makes us possibility thinkers. Imagine a high-level management meeting where leaders are eagerly assuming responsibility. Problems are noted, and leaders are motivated to respond, motivated to acknowledge their part in creating or perpetuating the problem. There are no but's. There are no excuses. There is no finger pointing. People are eager to help each other succeed.

You may read about my imagined leadership team and say: "Yeah, right. I'd love to work in a place like that, *but...*" If you are thinking that way, somebody (preferably yourself) needs to kick your *but.* Wherever we work, live or play, we are the creators of whatever is happening right now. Isn't it time that those of us who call ourselves leaders got off our *but's* and started leading? The joy of true success comes to those of us who are interested in leading a completely responsible life, and who can envision possible futures. The joy of true success comes to individuals and organizations who are willing to kick their *but's* and find the greatness that lies within them.

Summary: Challenge your *but's*. Complete responsibility will enhance joy and bring you closer to greatness.

5 The Vicious Cycle of Blaming

Blaming is circular. You put it out there and it comes back to you. You blame a colleague for a mistake. He gets angry at you and blames you for something. The conflict escalates as your anger and indignation increase. Let's take a look at how this vicious circle works. This illustration is explained on the next page.

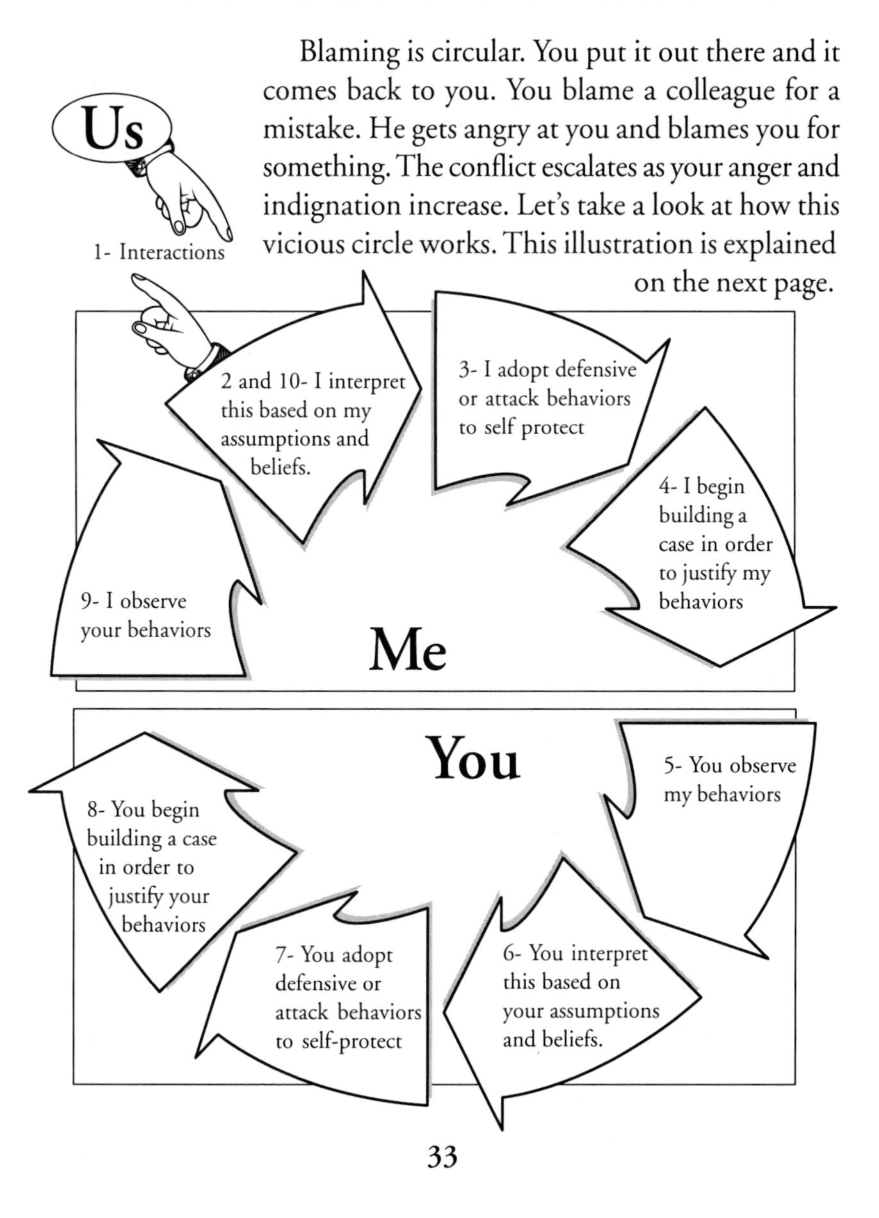

1. An interaction takes place between you and me. Words are spoken, an event takes place, or someone tells me something about you.

2. I interpret the interaction from my view of the world. I make assumptions about you based on my beliefs. Emotion is created by these thoughts. My assumptions have me feeling threatened by what I think you said or did.

3. I automatically begin self-protective behaviors. These may include avoiding you, verbally attacking you, talking to others about you, withholding information from you, ignoring your requests, or acting out in ways that demonstrate my irritation with you.

4. I begin looking for more "evidence" of your blame. This justifies my behavior.

5. You observe my behaviors or hear about them.

6. You make assumptions based on the behaviors you see. Emotion is created by these thoughts. You interpret my behavior as a threat to you.

7. You automatically begin self-protective behaviors. These may include avoiding me, verbally attacking me, talking to others about me, withholding information from me, ignoring my requests, or acting out in ways that demonstrate your irritation with me.

8. You begin looking for more "evidence" of my blame. This justifies your behavior.

9. I see your behaviors or hear about them.

10. My assumptions, beliefs, and interpretations are reinforced. I have more "evidence" for my case against you. This leads to more self-protecting behaviors. The cycle continues and escalates.

Remember Cindy and Gena from Chapter Two? Let's use them as an example. Gena has a dominant personality and tends to be aggressive in her approach to others. Cindy is more laid back in the behavior she presents to others, yet tends to be tense and easily feels hurt if she is criticized.

1. Gena discovers a mistake that Cindy has made in the data she has compiled. She is upset about it and, to herself, questions Cindy's competence. Gena approaches Cindy and says: "You've made a mistake." Her irritation and judgment toward Cindy come through in her tone of voice. She is standing over Cindy who is seated at her desk.

2. Cindy is surprised at the interruption and uncomfortable that Gena is standing over her and so close. Her interpretation is that she is being attacked and she feels threatened. She immediately defends herself saying that she looked over the numbers several times. She sees Gena as pushy and rude.

3. Cindy protects herself by not giving any credibility to Gena's presentation. She focuses her attention on keeping herself safe by adjusting her body to put some distance between them. Her mind is racing, thinking of all the reasons why she is competent and professional. She is not really hearing the words Gena is saying. Gena tells her she has already corrected the mistake.

4. When Gena walks away, Cindy feels both fearful and angry. She tells herself that Gena obviously doesn't like her and has judged her. She tells herself that Gena is overbearing and bossy. This justifies not respecting her or listening to her. As the days and the weeks pass, Cindy looks for more examples to prove that Gena is pushy and rude, and that she doesn't care about Cindy.

5. Gena sees that Cindy is not receiving her message. She finds Cindy to be defensive.

6. For Gena, Cindy's behavior reinforces her first thought—that Cindy is incompetent. Gena decides that Cindy probably can't do the job right. This thought angers her. She tells herself that Cindy is a problem. Gena sees Cindy as incompetent, uncooperative, and a poor listener.

7. "Why did they hire someone like this?" she asks herself. "Can't we ever get a competent person in this position?" She feels justified in her thoughts, because Cindy is, to her, obviously incompetent. She finds an ally in her friend, Sherry. Together they exchange critical remarks about Cindy.

8. Gena begins looking for more evidence of Cindy's incompetence and lack of cooperation. One day she sees Cindy studying at her desk for her night class. Gena sees this behavior as evidence that Cindy doesn't care about doing the job right. She is studying on company time! She presents disapproving looks to Cindy from across the room. She feels justified in complaining to Sherry.

9. Cindy observes and interprets Gena's behaviors.

10. Cindy sees the disapproving looks and receives some more criticism about mistakes she has made. This reinforces her negative opinion of Gena. This leads to more self-protecting behaviors.

As you can see, both women are caught up in their respective contexts and unable to understand each other. Neither has an understanding of how she affects the other. Each believes she is looking at reality, yet each is lost in the Vicious Cycle of Blaming. Unless Gena and Cindy are willing to question their assumptions about each other, the conflict will continue.

Another example:

1. I'm chairing a meeting and you are 10 minutes late. This is the third time you have been late. We have to review what was said for your benefit.

2. I interpret your tardiness as being inconsiderate of our time, not caring enough about the meeting, and assigning my meeting a low priority. This leads me to the assumption that you are arrogant and selfish.

3. I become less responsive to you because I think you don't deserve it. I assign your requests a low priority. Since you have quite a bit of influence in the organization, I don't confront you directly. I avoid you. I talk to a few of my trusted colleagues about what an arrogant jerk you are.

4. I look for other ways that prove you are a jerk. I am building a case for blame against you. This case justifies my lack of responsiveness to you, my avoidance, and my talking to others about you. I do not see my behaviors toward you as negative or unprofessional. I see what I think and do as justified. You have become the enemy. You are not a person to me, but an object of blame. You are something to be changed or removed.

5. You notice some of these negative behaviors or hear about them from others.

6. You interpret my slow response, my avoidance, and my talking about you as weakness and incompetence. You assume that I am not worthy of your time and concern. This creates more irritation for you as you think: "Who is he, that incompetent wimp, to complain about me?"

7. You protect yourself from my complaints by making sure you are late for my meetings, delaying or refusing to respond to my requests, and making cutting remarks to me in front of others.

8. You build your case by looking for more examples of my weakness and incompetence. This justifies your thoughts and behaviors. You do not see your behaviors as negative or unprofessional. You see what you think and do as justified. I have become the enemy. I am not a person to you, but an object of blame. I am something to be changed or removed.

9. I observe your behaviors.

10. My original assumptions are reinforced. You are arrogant. You are selfish. You are a jerk.

I escalate my efforts to prove what a jerk you are. When you arrive late at my meetings I am irritated, but I also find it satisfying. I expect you to be late. I am irritated, conflicted, distracted, and stressed. But I am also strangely satisfied, because at least I know that I am right about you. You have fulfilled my expectations.

The Vicious Cycle of Blaming is destined to continue as long as we each think the other is to blame. At some point it may explode into a full blown yelling match. If we yell at each other without being interrupted by onlookers, we may just have a chance of working out our differences. Through our expressed anger we will begin to see each other as real people with real needs and concerns. We will develop a respect for each others' boundaries. A bond can be created through our honest expression.

This is not a recommendation for yelling at each other to solve conflicts. It is an acknowledgment that sometimes it works. Sometimes, when people get their feelings out on the table, they begin to see each other. The honest expression of emotion can create a bond if it results in honest self-reflection, a willingness to admit to one's own faults, and the courage to speak openly.

Most people are unwilling to confront directly. Personal fears, fear of job loss, fear of authority, and fears about looking foolish get in the way of honest expression. Instead we go tell someone else, often hoping to get them on our side. We find ourselves analyzing the other person, explaining their motives, and convincing ourselves that is just the way they are. The problem is, we are making it all up. If we haven't talked directly with another person, how can we know? How do we know for sure about motives and reasons? How do we know the impact we are having on them? It is important to communicate directly with other people.

Direct communication doesn't necessarily mean direct confrontation. Direct confrontation about issues is not always necessary. Often it is our own assumptions that we need to confront rather than the other person. Direct confrontation from a blaming approach rarely works well. Direct communication given clearly and compassionately often does work well. Moving beyond blaming in our communication toward others requires us to understand the difference between content and context.

Try this: Think of someone you have a conflict with or that you have blamed for something.

- What assumptions do you hold about this person? Assumptions may include adjectives such as: incompetent, lazy, inconsiderate, stupid, arrogant, uncaring, or selfish.

- How do these assumptions have you behaving?

- How do you protect yourself from the threat this person seems to pose?

- Have you built a strong case against this person?

- How do you think this person sees you?

- How have your assumptions and behaviors affected them?

- What assumptions might they have made about you?

- Looking at your assumptions, your behavior, and your conversations to or about this person, how are these strategies working?

- Are you getting the results you really want?

Mary is constantly late. Jenny, her supervisor, is frustrated with the tardiness. She sees Mary as disorganized, inconsiderate of others at work, and as not caring about the organization. Her focus on her image of Mary as disorganized, inconsiderate, and uncaring prevents her from being effective. She is not dealing with Mary and she is not dealing with the problem. First, why is Mary late? Is there a factor in Mary's life that makes her unavoidably late? Is there a big problem in Mary's life? If there is a problem, what adjustments can be made? If there is not a big problem, Jenny needs to deal with the problem at hand.

Jenny needs to explain to Mary the impact of her tardiness on the organization and the importance of her being on time. She needs to clearly express her expectations. She needs to explain the consequences of continued tardiness. The assumptions Jenny has made are not real, nor are Mary's imagined faults the real problem. The problem is the tardiness. Mary is a real person who needs to be approached with respect, concern, and honesty. Jenny has enabled the tardiness by complaining and blaming. Once blaming is out of the way, Jenny can respond to the person and the problem.

Summary: Blaming leads to more blaming. The vicious cycle of blaming perpetuates itself. The cycle can only be broken by challenging your own assumptions.

6 Context and Content

Most of us can see by now that blaming doesn't make things better. We see how blaming disempowers us, hurts us, and stifles growth. We know that it really doesn't feel good when we are in a blaming environment. We also know that most of us are prone to keep on blaming. How do we move beyond blaming? How do we unleash all that power and passion that is within us? It begins with an understanding of content and context.

Each moment of life has content. People, places, activities, objects, communications, all make up the content of life. Content is what we draw upon when someone asks: "What happened?"

It is rare that anyone can describe what happened without adding one's own interpretation to it. Interpretation comes in the form of adjectives and adverbs, similes and metaphors, descriptive verbs and nouns. Interpretation comes from our context. All reality is experienced within a context. One's context comes from past experience, conditioning, culture, values, assumptions, and beliefs. Our context is our mental model of the world. Everything we experience is given a meaning. The meaning we give a situation *is* the experience we have.

Context is the hidden factor for most people. Most people see content, interpret it, and call it reality. It is their reality. We do not see the world as it is. We see the world as we are. Without an awareness of context we look at our "reality" and say: "That's the way it is." With an awareness of context we realize that reality is fluid. It can be shaped and changed.

Certainly we can change perceived reality for people through manipulation. Politicians, marketing professionals, and the news media do it every day. Many of the beliefs held by the public are given to us. Is the president doing a good job? Often the answer is dependent upon the public relations efforts of the president's staff and of those who oppose him. Do we really know if he is doing a good job? What are our criteria?

Look around at the people in your life. Who do you like and who do you dislike? Who is doing a good job and who is doing poorly? Who is helpful to you and who is not? Your answers to these questions come from context—your own biased perceptions. Most people believe it comes from content— hard, unquestionable fact. A person didn't help me in this particular instance, therefore she is not helpful. Most of us have a list of all the people who are good or bad based on whether they did or didn't behave acceptably in the past. In all of our judgments there is at least one missing piece. That piece is: "What impact did I have on this result?"

Events (content) happen in the world. Experience (context) happens within us. We create our experience. There is an old story that exemplifies this point. A reporter interviewed three baseball umpires to ascertain how they called balls and strikes. He asked the first umpire: "Sir, how do you call balls and strikes? How do you know?" The umpire thought a moment and responded: "I call each pitch the way I see it. It is what it is." He asked a second umpire the same question. He stated that he, too, called them the way he saw them. The reporter asked a third umpire the same question: "Sir, how do you call balls and strikes?"

"Well, son, it's like this. That pitch isn't anything until I say what it is. It's my call!"

This is true of everything that is thrown at you. It's not anything until you say what it is. Was it good? Was it bad? It's your call. This is context. If something is bothering you, you can recontextualize it. Look at it differently. Here is an example of what I mean.

I was driving to a workshop. Traffic was heavy. Some people were driving too slowly for me and some were driving hesitantly. "Move it!"

I shouted from within my car. "Get going! Do you drive much or what?" Of course, only my ears could hear this. After several minutes of extreme irritation and negative commentary, I stopped myself. "What is going on with me? Why am I getting so upset? These people aren't driving this way to hurt me. They are just doing the best they can to get where they want to go. They are no different from me." I recognized that these people were the target of my anger, not the cause. This realization changed my context. It was no longer me being a victim of all these "incompetent" drivers. Changing my context changed my experience. I was now calmly driving to my destination among hundreds of others driving to their destinations. We were sharing the roads. I became more considerate to other drivers. The drive became more pleasant. It wasn't any faster, but then, it wasn't going to be any faster if I yelled either.

In this new calm I asked myself why I was so upset. I had just left my workout at the local YMCA. Three days previous I had left my wallet unattended in a locker for a few minutes. It was taken by a young man along with my credit cards and $100 in cash. I was angry at the YMCA staff for not screening people properly. I was angry at the young man and wanted him to be caught. My unresolved anger had been sparked by my visit to the YMCA that morning. I realized that my wishes for the staff and that young man were unattainable goals. I was really angry at myself for leaving the wallet in an unlocked locker. I began to laugh at my foolishness. I let it all go with the intention to be more careful with where I left my personal things. I thought the problem was the "stupid" drivers around me. I thought it was the "stupid" YMCA staff. In reality I was angry at "stupid" me for leaving the wallet in an unlocked locker.

In my example reality was fluid. I went from discomfort and irritation, to calm, to humor and to insight. The facts of my reality remained the same. Hundreds of people were still driving to their destinations. It was how I experienced that situation that changed. However, my shift in my personal reality did affect everyone else.

What if I had allowed my anger to increase? What if I became so impatient that I began zipping in and out of the traffic, cutting people off, and eventually causing an accident? Now the facts have changed. Instead of hundreds of drivers steadily making progress toward their respective destinations, we now have a few banged up cars, maybe some people with minor injuries, and the arrival of two police cars. Now many of these people are going to be late for work, or not show up at all. Customers, co-workers, managers, and others who are served by these people in the traffic jam will be affected. I have just made life a little more difficult for hundreds, maybe thousands, of people.

Would I have learned anything from this? Would I be sitting in my banged up car knowing I had allowed my blaming and anger to cause this accident? Or, I could be sitting there saying: "If it weren't for all these stupid drivers I wouldn't be in this mess!"

Every day we make decisions from our context that affect the world. We all participate in and affect reality. Reality is not something that happens to us. We create our personal reality and we affect the collective reality that surrounds us. We affect reality in ways we may never understand. To a person who clearly understands context, there can be no such thing as blame. In my example from Chapter Five, I am part of the vicious cycle of blaming. I blame my colleague for being late to my meeting without being aware that I am influencing his reality. I believe that it is something happening *to* me, when, in fact, it is happening *in* me. I am unable to see how my thoughts and emotions shape my experience. I am unwilling to see how my thoughts and emotions affect my colleague.

The key to personal power is understanding context. Imagine you are watching a movie in a theater. Just as the story reaches a good part, suddenly, the camera moves, and all the action is obscured by a big rock right in the middle of the picture. The picture stays this way, with the rock preventing you from seeing anything that's happening, and ruining the movie. Your experience is really suffering from it being there. Do you get mad at the rock? Do you blame the rock for ruining your afternoon? It is the only thing preventing you from seeing the good part of the movie. Of course you don't get mad at the rock, because you know, despite the unquestionable fact that the rock is the only thing in your way, that the director of the movie chose to put the camera behind the rock. So do you blame the director? Here's the problem we run into: in your own life, in the private screening room in your mind where you watch and re-watch the situations in your life, you are the director. Regardless of what happens in it, only you decide how you perceive your life. While it seems ridiculous to blame the rock while watching someone else's movie, it's easy to blame the rock when you're watching your own. It's easy not to acknowledge that you chose to set the scene that way. It's easy to forget that you had other choices in your handling of that moment.

You select certain thought forms and project them on your screen. A rock obscuring the picture is a metaphor for your view of the world. In situations where you feel slighted or picked on, it is your view of the world that has you creating that experience. When you feed the emotion with repetitive, blaming thoughts, you create the drama.

2500 years ago, a spiritual master called the Buddha was being "insulted" by some onlookers. He did not respond to them. One of his followers asked: "Why do you let these people insult you? Why don't you say something?" The Buddha replied: "If someone gives you a gift, and you do not receive it, to whom does it belong?" We cannot be attacked unless we feel attacked.

As I stated in Chapter One, the world is filled with self-righteous indignation. So many people and groups of people are looking for reasons to be insulted, to be outraged, to be upset. Our indignation comes from within our own minds. The next time you feel attacked, insulted, or slighted, ask yourself: "Why am I choosing to feel this way? How does it benefit me? What do I really want from this situation?" You can spend your life waiting for someone to change or apologize or you can get on with life.

The need for someone else to do something in order for you to feel better disempowers you. It is understandable that you may be angry. It is understandable that you may feel hurt, rejected, disappointed, or betrayed. I would never tell someone they shouldn't feel the way they do. The question is: Do you want to continue feeling this way? Are you willing to do something about it? If you are willing to change the situation, you begin by examining your context. As Dr. Steven Covey wrote in his book, *The 7 Habits of Highly Effective People*: "How we *see* the problem *is* the problem."

Defining another person as "the problem" or even a past event as "the problem" is not useful. We cannot change other people, nor can we change past events. We can only change the context in which we experience those people and events. If we are not focusing our energy on what we can change, our thoughts and actions in this present moment, then we are focusing on blaming.

If I am caught in a rainstorm in the middle of a golf course, my problem is not the rainstorm. I can contemplate rainstorms, blame them, rail at them, or yell at the sky. I can criticize myself for not anticipating the storm, for taking this risk, or for not getting an electric cart. None of these thoughts defines or solves my problem. My problem is: How do I safely and quickly transport myself to a destination that is dry and safe from the storm? In this situation, the rain, the thunder, the lightning, the terrain, my golf equipment, and my body make up the content. Fears, regrets, and worry make up my context. Feeling victimized by the storm, by my physical body's limitations, or by any reasons why I happen to have been golfing at that time are all context.

In order to solve my problem I may need to break my context. One way of doing that is to bring my thinking into the present moment. I face the facts of the situation. Instead of resisting the situation, I respond to it. I ask myself what I want and what I need to do right now to achieve it. Two years ago when I was in this situation I stopped myself from wishing the storm had come later, wishing I had come earlier, and blaming myself for insisting on playing another hole when the sky was getting dark. It was raining hard and I wanted to be safe and dry. I headed directly toward the nearest shelter to wait out the storm.

People do not get angry at facts so much as they get angry at the meaning they attach to the facts. If my gas gauge is on empty, it is unlikely that I will be angry at the gas gauge. I need to face facts and act. Anger and blaming are often symptoms that we are resisting reality, not accepting it.

On my drive from the YMCA, my context of wishing and blaming had me *resisting* reality. I broke my context by focusing on the present moment. In that moment I was *responding* to my reality. I responded to my anger by recognizing it and asking myself why. I saw that my anger made no sense and that it put both myself and others at risk. As emotions subsided, I noticed what was really going on. People were driving to destinations. The only way I could be assured that I got to mine as quickly and safely as possible, was if everyone else moved toward their respective destinations quickly and safely, too.

Responsiveness to our reality is powerful. Resistance to our reality makes us powerless. Blaming is always a form of resistance. When our context has us resisting reality the context must be broken. Whenever we are in an emotional state we can ask: "What is happening right now? How am I feeling about it? What can I do about it? Is what I'm thinking or doing right now helping to make it better or worse? What results am I desiring? What should I do next to move toward those results?"

Power comes from your ability to change your context. There must be a willingness to let go of the present context. If you are feeling victimized, your emotional tendency will be to hold on to your suffering. Yet, is this what you want? Do you want to stay in a state of hurt or anger? You can make the decision that you have had enough of being a victim. You are only a victim as long as you think of yourself as one. When you decide that you are no longer a victim, that no one is to blame, you become more powerful.

Summary: Our experience of the world happens within our own minds. We tend to blame others for conditions that we are creating in our minds. Power comes from our ability to change our context.

7 Breaking Context

If we are blaming, our context is distorted. We are seeing things in a way that makes us feel we are right, victimized, or the only one who matters, but we are failing to see reality in a way that truly serves us. The blaming emotions of hurt, anger, bitterness, resentment, or disgust are signals that we have a problem. I am not saying it is wrong to have these emotions. Nor am I saying these emotions are not justified. I am saying these emotions signal that we have a problem. These emotions, in most cases, tell us that we are resisting reality. We are resisting other people's needs. As long as we are in resistance, we will not be able to resolve any issue. We break context by having the awareness that our negative emotions are distorted. They do not tell us the truth about the situation.

I once worked with a sporting goods distribution company. I found that the sales people were always complaining about the purchasing people. Likewise, the purchasing people complained that the sales people had no idea of what purchasing was about. Blaming was expressed, but they never openly expressed their blaming thoughts to each other. They were frustrated with each other and at times angry.

One day I asked a simple question: "Do you guys ever talk?" The purchasing people said that of course they talked. They greeted people, asked about their families, and occasionally conversed about changes in the business. "No!" I said, "I mean, do you ever talk? Do you discuss purchasing and sales strategy? When you see a great deal on a bulk purchase of products, does Purchasing ask

Sales if they think they can sell it? Do you meet regularly with each other to discuss problems and opportunities, to give and receive suggestions, and to plan together?"

They answered that they never met with each other. In this company Sales and Purchasing had no real relationship. Rather than inquiring, they guessed at each others' thinking. When problems arose they blamed each other. Although they attended plenty of management meetings together, they never met specifically to discuss their plans. One way to break context is to stop guessing and ask. Stop assuming what others think or want, and go ask them.

There is a tendency for people in groups to blame other groups. People make negative assumptions and decide that the other group is uncooperative, unintelligent, or difficult. Once we make negative assumptions about another group, it becomes impossible for us to understand them. Having made our assumptions, we think we already know all that there is to know about the other group. They are uncooperative, therefore everything they do and say is placed within the framework of "uncooperative".

In other words, "uncooperative" becomes our context for seeing the other group. Whatever they say or do, we will shape it into an uncooperative experience in our minds. Negative opinions must always be justified. We justify our opinions by continuously searching for evidence to support them. As we build our case against the other group, we step further outside the lines of civility, teamwork, and caring. Negative humor, putdowns, and sarcasm become our way of speaking about the other group. Our conversation about the other group is disrespectful, but it is justified in our minds.

When groups hold very different opinions, they often stop listening to one another. Points of view become adversarial-- us and them. Since our group is right, anything their group says has no merit. We comment on their lack of intelligence, their insane views, and their immoral behavior. Instead of an intelligent dialogue between opposing points of view, we have name calling and blaming. In the United States, conservative talk radio hosts have utilized this kind of blaming to further their own agendas. The word "liberal", for example, is no longer descriptive of a set of viewpoints. Many conservatives in the USA now use the word as a putdown. "He's a liberal. Oh! That explains everything!" In the late 1960s, many liberals in the US did the same thing. All conservatives were characterized as racists and rednecks.

This kind of thinking creates polarization between groups. Differing points of view and different goals become a reason for blaming. We feel blaming is justified because our group's goals and our group's viewpoints are right. With this kind of justification there is no dialogue. With no dialogue the only option is force. We attempt to force others to comply through verbal attack, policy changes, manipulation, legislation, or war. In the blaming mode we think others should change because we are right, they are wrong, or we know better. If they do not wish to change, then there must be something wrong with them. They feel the same way toward us.

In this polarized state the other side is not real to us. They are not real people. Their opinions and beliefs do not matter. Their needs are irrelevant. To us, they are objects to be moved. We resist their reality. We don't want to know their reality, so we invent it in our minds. We create an image of the other side and that becomes our reality. The image may seem real to us, but that doesn't make it the truth.

Two thousand years ago another great teacher called the Christ said the following: "Before you would remove the speck from your brother's eye, first remove the beam from your own eye. This will help you to see more clearly."

Breaking context is removing this beam that blocks our vision. We often cannot see the truth because we distort it with our invented reality. When we resist another person or group, we cannot see them. We begin to see when we allow others to be real. Allowing reality means that we recognize the needs and concerns of others and we give importance to them. We then respond to the other person or group by listening to them with the intent to understand. "...grant that I may not so much seek to be consoled as to console, to be understood as to understand ...", St. Francis wrote in his famous prayer. Or, as Stephen Covey wrote in *The*

7 Habits of Highly Effective People: "Seek first to understand, and then to be understood."

Understanding another person or group does not mean agreeing with them. It does not mean condoning their behavior nor does it mean being polite about it. We break context by moving from judging to discerning. To judge is to offer blame, guilt, or condemnation. To discern is to see clearly. We usually do not help people by judging them. We help them by seeing them clearly, helping them to see themselves more clearly, and helping them to see the results they are producing.

As a coach, I do not judge a manager who is harsh toward his colleagues and employees. I may discern that his way of being is ineffective, hurtful, and costly to the organization. I do not see the "harsh" manager as a bad person, but I may see him as someone who is behaving badly. Were I to judge him, how would my condemnation make him a better leader? How would my judgment build a positive working relationship with him? It is likely that my judgment would invite resistance on his part. I would be inviting him to dig in and defend his position.

Instead of judging, I can recognize that his way of being comes out of his context. The only way to help him is to assist him in breaking his context. He believes that his way of being produces good results. His way of managing is his response to reality as he sees it. My first step is to understand him. My second step is to show him what results he is really producing. By surveying his employees and colleagues, I compile data on his impact as a leader and communicator. He may argue about the "rightness" of his way of being, but he cannot argue with results.

I have found that success varies depending on the willingness of the leader to honestly self-reflect. When we suddenly discover we are negatively affecting others, that we are blaming others for situations we are causing, and that we are not as "right" as we thought we were, it can be painful. I have seen leaders immediately change their context upon finding out what a negative effect they were having on others. The pain in these cases is good. It motivates people to respond.

I held a corporate position years ago where I worked closely with people. I facilitated team building at various locations, built bridges between people, and helped to improve communication. Although I facilitated and taught these skills well, I had a huge blind spot that was a great impediment to my success.

A new chief operating officer was hired who spotted it right away. He took me aside and expressed that he had a concern to discuss. He went on to explain that I often said things that were intended as humor, but were not taken that way. He gave an example of a remark I had made to him. He explained that when I made the remark, I was the only one who was laughing. He told me that he had seen me do this with other people, too. My critical and sarcastic humor was actually very destructive to all of my working relationships. He said that he didn't think that was the result I was intending to produce, and that I might want to take a look at this behavior.

As I listened to him I felt embarrassed and horrified at myself. The other people who had been the recipients of my "humor" became very real to me. My context as the people person with the great sense of humor was broken. I saw myself instead as an insensitive person who had fun at the expense of others. This was painful. Suddenly, I understood why some people weren't very supportive of my goals. I thanked him and immediately changed who I was being. I stopped teasing people. I began looking for sincere positive things to say to others. I didn't do this to show them that I cared. I did it because I did care about them. Immediately I began to experience greater support from others in my workplace. Our ability to break context depends on our willingness to respond to what is really happening.

My manager helped me to break my context successfully. Had he judged me and accused me of making cutting remarks, I would have felt differently. I may have changed my behaviors, but not who I was being. I would have spent my days trying to behave better. It is unlikely that my relationships would have improved much, because my context would have been the same. I would have blamed him, the other employees, or myself. I would have been trying to show that manager that I had changed, that I cared about the others, and that what he thought about me wasn't true. In changing my context, I didn't have to try to improve. I just did it. We help others to break context by offering honest, compassionate feedback.

One of my clients was an extremely stressed-out manager who saw the job and the people he worked with as the cause of his stress. I collected data from his employees and colleagues. One thing that came up was his tendency to criticize customers and other leaders in the organization in front of his employees. He admitted that he did do that. We talked about what kinds of results he was producing with this behavior.

He began to see that he was teaching his employees to complain about and blame customers and leaders in other departments. He affected customer service in a negative way by blaming and teaching others to blame. He was undermining his own authority by blaming others and making himself appear powerless. His focus on things he could not change was creating stress. His "venting" about others in front of his employees was not de-stressing him, but creating more stress. As he talked to his employees about problem people he tended to become more angry. What he did not see was that he was a big problem to his employees.

Seeing himself in this way was a shock. His context as a victim changed. Not being a victim, he immediately stopped complaining and blaming in front of his employees. We can change context immediately if we are willing to give up being a victim. In moving from victim to victor, there was no longer any payoff in blaming. Those he had blamed became real people with real needs. His employees needed him to be a leader, an example of how to respond to both internal and external customers. They needed his help in solving their problems, not to be a sounding board for his problems. Other leaders and customers needed him to listen and to take effective action.

Sometimes, no matter how much respect and understanding you offer, no matter how discerning your observations may be, people will still resist you. Actually they are resisting themselves. They are unwilling to stop judging and blaming. They are unwilling to self-reflect. They are unwilling to give up being a victim. They are unwilling to see clearly how they affect others. In my coaching experience, these people usually end up being moved to another position or out of the organization. We cannot make others change, and we need not blame them. However, choices have consequences. It is important not to protect people from their own consequences.

Often the story in organizations is that we blame and judge, but don't act. If we do act, it seems only to create a mess including hard feelings, lawsuits, and painful terminations. Despite how impossible some situations may seem to be, and how much suffering they may put upon us, we are not the victims of poor managers or poor employees, or bad situations. Our inability to communicate directly, to discern, to offer honest feedback, and to give up blaming causes us to create and perpetuate these situations. We can only successfully deal with the negative actions of others if we deal with ourselves first. Our first step is to stop deceiving ourselves.

Summary: Once we understand context, we realize we don't have to change the world. Our ability to question negative assumptions, and to give up being a victim, will have us creating more desirable results.

8 Self-Deception And Blaming

Self-deception is something most of us do not think about. When we blame we are so convinced of another's faults that it usually doesn't occur to us that we could be creating the problem. Self-deception is about walking around with that big beam in our collective eye but not being aware of it. Think of someone you have known who was selfish, uncaring, and caused trouble for others. Did that person know that she had a problem? In most cases the answer would be "No!" You might remember a time when you were the one who caused trouble and didn't know it. One day you woke up, or somebody woke you up, and you saw what you had done. In that moment, the people you had hurt became very real to you.

How do we get ourselves into this state of self-deception? *Leadership and Self-Deception*, a book by the Arbinger Institute, offers insight into this question. It's a great book and I recommend that you read it. The book tells us that there are only two ways to be with people. We are either responsive or resistant. When we respond we see others as real people with real needs and concerns. When we resist we see people as objects. Arbinger defines objects as one of three things: something that helps you reach your goals, something that seems to be a barrier to your goals, or something that is irrelevant to your goals. In the resistant state we see others in a systematically distorted way. We see others in terms of our own needs and our own goals. In my driving to the workshop experience, people in other cars were objects to me. I was not concerned whether or not they arrived at their destinations. My only concern was getting to my destination, and they were in my way.

In my life as an executive who made "humorous" remarks to others, I did not fully consider their needs. I was satisfying my need for humor and attention. People who were the targets of my humor were objects, but I didn't know that. I saw myself as very considerate of others.

In our conflicts with others we tend to justify our blaming and our behavior with our "rightness". When I think I am completely right, I am unwilling to consider what the other person needs, thinks, cares about, or wants. The other person senses that I do not really care about his needs. My blaming encourages him to blame me. My unwillingness to listen encourages him not to listen. As we each assert our positions, we distance ourselves from each other and a mutually agreeable solution.

Why do we resist each other? Why do we deceive ourselves that others are the problem? Arbinger suggests the problem lies in self-betrayal. Arbinger defines self-betrayal as: "1. An act contrary to what I feel I should do for another is an act of self-betrayal. 2. When I betray myself, I begin to see the world in a way that justifies my self-betrayal. " (The Arbinger Institute, *Leadership and Self-Deception*)

We each know what it means to be a person. We have a sense of what we need. Often we have a sense for what others need. When we resist this sense, this inner knowing, we betray ourselves. When we betray ourselves we feel the need to justify ourselves. We recreate reality to align with the image of ourselves that we want to have. We remember situations in a way that justifies our own thinking and behavior.

Jerry runs a department in an organization. Some knowledge comes to him that would greatly benefit his counterpart, Rob, in another department. His first thought is: "This information would really give them an edge. I should call Rob right away." His good intention is quickly overshadowed by other needs and concerns. He thinks to himself: "I don't have time. I have a lot to do." The day passes and he doesn't deliver the information.

The next day he sees that the advantage is now lost. He did not act on his first thought, which was to offer the information. In not following his intuition, and not doing what he knew to be the right thing, he betrayed myself. Seeing himself in this way is unpleasant. He begins to justify his lack of action. He tells himself that he's a good manager. He needed to take care of his own department first. He had to focus on tasks A, B, and C and couldn't do anything else. He thinks: "Rob doesn't go out of his way to help me, so why should I help him? Why should I make him look good, when he doesn't care about my department? Besides, if he was on the ball, he would have found this information himself. Obviously, he's not too bright." Jerry begins to think of past interactions that "prove" Rob was undeserving of the information he had.

Suddenly, taking care of certain issues in his own department has taken on greater urgency. Suddenly, Rob has become so bad he is not worthy of Jerry's respect. When Jerry had the thought: "This information would really give them an edge. I should call him right away." Was Rob such a bad guy? Were Jerry's tasks so overwhelming when he had that thought? It seems that Rob's negative characteristics became a factor after Jerry failed to give him the information. It seems that his tasks increased in importance after he failed to give him the information.

You might ask: "What if Jerry was right? Maybe Rob isn't too bright. Maybe Jerry's tasks are overwhelming at this moment? Maybe Rob wouldn't help Jerry out if the situation were reversed." All of this may be true. None of it erases the fact that Jerry had a thought, an inner urge, to offer Rob the information. None of this erases the fact that Jerry betrayed that feeling. If Jerry's failure to act hurts Rob's department, it also hurts the organization.

The image Jerry builds of himself as a hardworking manager is at Rob's expense. In order to justify himself Jerry has to make Rob bad or incompetent. The more "bad" Jerry could make him appear to be, the more "good" Jerry could attribute to himself. Now he has himself in a position where doing the "wrong" thing is justified. He thinks: "I'm the kind of manager who works hard for this organization." Instead of dealing with his self betrayal, he blames it on Rob. He is resistant to Rob's needs and concerns. Rob is not a real person to

Jerry. Jerry's focus is on maintaining his image as a hard working manager who is very busy. This is his story.

Self-betrayal leads to self-portrayal. Jerry portrays himself as the hard-working manager. His story is so important to him he is unable to see his impact on others. When bad things happen, he is not responsible, because he is a hard-working manager. It is always them. In externalizing all problems and issues, he avoids reality. People may think he is not such a good manager, but he is resistant to their opinion. He tells himself that he is not here to be liked. Or, he sees himself as the unappreciated victim of people who don't really know him.

His self-justifying image (his story) becomes a way of life. There is an intuitive feeling that tells him the right thing to do, and often, he is not even aware of it. His self justifying image causes him to be defensive. His time and energy is spent justifying and managing the image. He may be technically effective, a wealth of knowledge in his field. He may be a great problem-solver with his knowledge. He may be a visionary in terms of what his department can achieve. He may be competent in many ways, but his tendency to blame, to treat people as objects, will trip him up. This is self-deception.

Jerry's focus on justifying his story takes him out of this present moment. He is unable to see the potential in this present moment. His inability to see how his way of being hurts others prevents him from growing, and from being effective with others. He is unable to respond effectively to other people. The person he is being doesn't care about others. He may tell himself he cares, because that's part of his story. His story of himself as the hard working manager and who he is really being are not in alignment. Others can see this, but he can't. He has created a mental structure that automatically projects his way of being onto others. He creates a world where he is right and others are wrong.

Living from his story, his eyes do not see and his ears do not hear. They simply make his world agreeable to his story about himself. His mind takes what he sees and hears and translates it into a form that is agreeable to him. Sometimes a thought breaks through that challenges his blaming reality, or a feeling to help someone. He sees a way to truly help an "enemy". He suddenly knows what he can do or say to help his spouse feel more loved. He knows what to do or say to help his co-worker feel more confident. He immediately doubts his sanity and quickly retreats into his story. He tells himself that they don't deserve it, or that he would be too vulnerable if he expressed that feeling. He continually betrays himself.

He says he is willing to admit mistakes. He says that he is willing to look at himself. He is so good at deceiving himself, so conditioned into seeing the world in this distorted way, that he cannot fathom that the problem is him. His efforts are spent justifying his acts to prove to himself and to the world that he really is that kind of person. His story becomes his context for seeing the world. He relies on force, because in this context, he has no real power.

You probably recognize Jerry. You have worked with him or he is a member of your family. He is you and he is me. There may always be times when we blame. We are lost in the downward spiral of self deception when we are focused on how we're right and we're justified, and others are wrong. We need not judge ourselves for this. It is human. We break out of the self-deception of blaming by understanding that our context is distorted.

In order to break context we must begin to question our own virtue. The blame game is on if I am building my case against others while insisting on my own virtue. If I am focusing my energy on counting all the ways that I am right, good, justified, or better than another, then I am in the game. I can question my assumptions about myself. I can begin to face reality with these questions:

- Have I betrayed myself in any way?

- Have I broken promises to myself or another?

- Have I violated my own values and sense of what is right?

- Have I been honest with others?

- Have I attempted to mislead others in any way?
- Am I doing anything that has a negative impact on others?
- Am I spending my thoughts and energy justifying myself?

Self-betrayal, as presented here, makes the assumption that we each have an Inner Voice or feeling that helps us to know the right thing to do. Someone approaches a door that we are approaching. We feel an urge to open the door for them. We see a child who is discouraged. We feel an urge to offer an encouraging word. This feeling could be called conscience, or intuition, or a message from our Inner Being. It may show up as an urge, feeling, or a conscious thought. Do we all have this Inner Voice? Do we all have this inner messaging system? Would it be a safe assumption to say that we all have the potential to develop and/or attune to this voice? I believe we do.

The idea of intuition is not new. Intuition is knowing without knowing how you know. You just know. In the example Jerry knew to offer that information to Rob. He didn't do it. He betrayed what he knew he should do. Self-betrayal doesn't feel good. In order to feel better, we justify it. Like Jerry, we project the blame onto someone else. In a moment of frustration I may make a negative remark to my spouse. She reacts with another negative remark. I get angry at her reaction. In my mind I have an instant of knowing that my remark was impatient and inconsiderate. I have a flash of understanding about her reaction. I understand why I am irritated.

I feel or know an apology would bring us closer. That's my Inner Voice. Instead I walk away, blaming her. I tell myself, "She never apologizes to me!" I build my case, complaining about her treatment of me. I think of all the ways that I am a good husband. I think of all that I am receiving from her that I don't deserve. Later, I expect her to break the ice. When she doesn't, I double my blaming. By now I have forgotten my Inner Voice.

In this way we bury the intuitive voice that is within us. For many, this Inner Voice is buried by so much blaming it is seldom, if ever, heard or felt. We invest so much emotional energy protecting our image of self that we lose sight of who we are. As the offended spouse my energy is caught up in being the victim. I am so caught up in my victimhood that I cannot see my partner. I cannot hear or feel the intuitive voice. I am busy protecting my view of myself.

An awareness of context and an awareness of who we are being can help us to sense the inner voice. We need to be aware when we are blaming and make the assumption that our negative thoughts and emotions are distorting reality. Start listening to yourself. Pause before you react. Question your assumptions about the other person.

- Are they as horrible as they seem?
- Does everyone experience them that way?
- Am I as virtuous as I seem?
- Has my behavior been as perfect as I portray it?
- What do I want to come of this?

We are each unique as human beings, yet we are the same. This similarity helps us to feel for others, to be compassionate. We see someone suffer, and a part of us suffers. We see someone experiencing total joy and we feel joy. We are connected through emotion. We see someone in trouble and we feel an urge to help. Not listening to this feeling is self-betrayal. It results in blaming. We either blame ourselves, or we blame others.

I'm driving down the highway, in a big hurry to get to an appointment. Someone is pulled over, waving for help. I have a feeling and a thought that I should stop. Then I worry about being late, about being involved in someone else's problems, so I drive on. Seeing them in my rearview mirror, I feel regret. I tell myself it was the right thing to do. I really didn't have time. I really didn't know that person. I feel guilty from my self-blame. My self-betrayal has me diminishing myself with guilt.

I'm at work, and a few people are joking about another employee. The humor is cruel and they are all laughing. I laugh, too, to fit in. Besides, it was funny. My intuitive voice said to speak up for that person, but I was afraid. I didn't want to be the next target. I justify my joining in the joke. "She probably deserves it," I tell myself. "If she didn't act and dress so strangely, people wouldn't talk that way about her. Why should I stick my neck out for someone who doesn't have the good sense to be a little more normal?" My self-betrayal has me diminishing others, and defending those who behave inappropriately.

I'm with a few of my colleagues, and we are bashing the most senior manager. Something about this doesn't feel right, but I like the laughter. My intuitive voice is saying that if I have a problem with him, I should address it with him. As entertaining as it seems, this behind the back bashing isn't healthy. I tell myself it doesn't matter; he wouldn't listen anyway. I blame him for me not being honest.

My betrayal has me being the victim. After a time, I forget about the intuitive voice, and I join in the bashing. It has become normal. I have convinced myself that I can't really do anything about my manager's incompetence, so I accept it as reality. My story is that I am a good manager, but I can only do so much. I don't have the power to make a difference.

Instead of bashing the boss, can I get to know him? What if he really isn't doing a good job? I can talk to him like he is a real person. I can show him the results of his actions. I can offer my help. I can make sure I do not enable poor management by going along, criticizing it, or joking about it. I can focus my thought and emotion on creating a healthy and successful environment.

The tendency to blame is decreased when we listen to our inner voice. I see that my spouse has had a difficult day. I feel or have a knowing that a hug would be helpful. The feeling is interrupted by another thought: "I had a hard day, too. I don't see her hugging me. If she really cared she would be offering me a hug." Now I have a choice. I can act on the inner voice, or I can retreat into my blaming.

Which option will serve my spouse best? Which will serve our relationship best? Which will serve me best? I decide to give the hug. I see that it helps her. At the same time, I feel better, too. My responsiveness to my spouse adds something to me. I learn that as I spend less time worrying about my needs, and more time responding to hers, that I feel better. My responsiveness to her invites her to respond to me.

As a consultant and leader, I always have to be aware of my tendency to want to change people. I cannot change or fix others. Most people resist changing when we are trying to get them to change. In trying to get someone to change I am seeing him as an object. His changing helps me to attain my goals. He resists me because my efforts are seen as an attack on him.

To be effective I must stop blaming him for the way he is and stop trying to change him for me. This is the shift in context. I stop blaming and I respond to him. I focus my attention on his needs, his concerns, and his goals. My intent shifts from helping me to helping him. I offer genuine concern and listening. I set aside what I think should happen and allow what is best to happen. In other words, I don't control the outcome. I trust that by being clear and responsive the outcome will be better than if I try to force it or control it. I cannot motivate another person. I can only create an environment where they may motivate themselves.

How do you get someone else to change? You don't. Your ability to offer genuine care and concern invites others to improve. Your ability to offer honest communication with the intent of giving help invites others to be honest. Others are influenced by your shift in being. At the very least, you see the situation more truthfully. As you offer genuine care and concern, as you begin to see more truthfully, your awareness of the inner voice increases. As you listen to your inner voice, others are encouraged to listen to theirs.

The key motivator in blaming is fear. You have to get control of your fears. Fear comes from being concerned about yourself. It comes from being immersed in your story. You think the image in your story is real, that it is really you. Any threat to the image brings out your fear. It seems like a fight for survival. It is only a fight for the survival of your image. Your defensiveness is not protecting you; it is protecting your story. Next time you feel defensive ask yourself: "What am I defending?" You will find that it is not you, but an image you want everyone to have of you.

For example, I am driving the car and my wife tells me to turn right. I snap back at her: "I know which way to turn. Let me drive, will you?" I am not really defending me because I am not under attack. I carry an image of myself as a smart driver, a guy who knows how to get to the destination. This story is being threatened. My wife's comment seems incongruent with my story. Doesn't she know I am a smart driver? Doesn't she know that I know the way? What is the matter with her?

The real question, of course, is what is the matter with me? Why am I so defensive? Why does that comment bother me so much? I don't like being thought of as not knowing what I am doing. My story is that I'm the kind of guy who has things under control. I can handle this driving thing. I'm a man. As I lash out at my wife she becomes my audience. I am wanting a certain response from her. I want her to agree with my story. What does she need? Does this cross my mind?

I find myself blaming her for not really knowing me. If she really knew me she wouldn't doubt my driving ability. Suddenly I stop my thoughts. I listen to my defensive reaction and feel a little foolish. I realize that she isn't attacking me. I am attacking myself with my thoughts. I tell her I am sorry for snapping at her. I ask her if she is worried about not getting to our destination. She says she isn't. She was just trying to be helpful.

Defensive reactions are evidence of self-justifying images at work. Defensiveness becomes our way of being and we feed it by repeating our story. My story is my reason for being upset. My story is a lie.

There is no attack. There is a guy driving and a woman who reminds him to turn right. Those are the facts. The meaning given those facts is made up by me. My fear is not real. There is no attack from which I must defend; only my image seems under attack.

Whenever you find yourself being defensive or feeling threatened come into this present moment and ask: "What can I change and what can't I change?" Take action to change what you can — your thoughts, your assumptions, your words, your actions. Accept the things that you cannot change—the behavior of others, certain conditions. It makes no sense to worry about what you cannot change. As you focus your attention on what you can change, you increase your power.

When fear grips our minds we cannot think clearly. Fear drives us into self-deception and blaming. As you let go of fear, you can think more clearly. Breathe. Let go. Be present. Stop all blaming. Step back. What is really happening? What does this person in front of me need? As you find a place of calm, your inner voice can be heard. Ideas come. You know what to do. I am constantly amazed at the wisdom that comes out of my mouth when I am calm, centered, and focused on the needs of those around me.

If you find yourself in the middle of fear, blaming a person or situation for what is happening, stop. Take a breath. Take charge of your mind. In your mind, ask for help. Follow the inner feeling you receive. Focus your attention on what others need.

In any group of people, the person who is most at peace, most clear about who they are and what they want, and most able to stop worrying about themselves and focus on the needs of others— this is the person with the most power. Most of us are trained to blame, feel like a victim, and be driven by fear. As you practice breaking that context, and finding your inner voice, you stop deceiving yourself. Without deception you can look upon yourself and others and truly see what is happening. You can become that most powerful person in a group.

As we meet the needs of others, they are more likely to help us meet our needs. When I think that certain people must meet my needs, I am, again, powerless. I meet the needs of others by listening, caring, and doing what I can to help. I cannot always give people what they want, but I can usually give them what they need.

When you find yourself in an emotional conflict with another be aware that self-deception is going on. You know that they are deceiving themselves. The only thing you can do about it is to stop deceiving yourself. Take your focus off your perceived needs and look at the person before you. Forget about your opinions for a moment and see the others as they are. What do you see? How are they experiencing you? Who are you being with them? What is needed right now to help this situation? Listen. Your ability to be in this moment and fully present with this person will create a shift in the conflict. You will move closer to improving the relationship and possibly a resolution, too.

Summary: We deceive ourselves when we think that others are the problem and we are not. Our willingness to see others not as objects but as real people, and be concerned about their needs, makes us more powerful. Our ability to hear and act on the Inner Voice has us responding truly rather than betraying ourselves.

9. Collusion in Conflict

Recently I heard a high-ranking Israeli official say that certain compromises needed to be made with the Palestinians. His reasoning was that the fighting will go on unless they get some of their problems addressed. He then qualified his statement by saying he didn't suggest this idea because he cared about the Palestinians. He added that frankly, he did not care about them. This is the heart of the problem. If the Palestinians' needs are of no concern; if he gives no value to their interests; then it will not matter what he offers them.

Despite what actions others take, we can tell whether they truly care about our needs or if they are just *dealing* with us like an inanimate problem. Others can see through us when we treat them as nothing more than a problem to be dealt with. In the case of the Israeli official, *nothing* he offers will be of value, because he does not value Palestinians as human beings. He does not see them as real people with needs and concerns as important as his own. You cannot create peace with others if you don't care about them. You may not like them, but you must care about them.

Consider this: anyone who has lived in a house has probably had to negotiate with a variety of neighbors over various things— noise levels for example. If you think back over your role in these sorts of incidents, you will probably find that you only felt the urge to do "the right thing" a certain amount of the time, but not all of the time. How do you respond differently to say, a neighbor who knocks on your door and asks you in a friendly way to make less noise, or a neighbor who simply yells out the window or calls the police to your house. Both of you have a legitimate need— you, to have fun in your own house, the neighbor, to get some peace and quiet. Regardless of whether you have anything in common with him or want to be his friend, how much stronger is your desire to help him get peace and quiet if he first shows some respect by not ruining your fun? How much more likely are you to make less noise in the future in each case? How much would you trust him in the future? How often would you talk to him? Would you handle future disagreements with respect for his needs? You would probably only do these things if you were a person of great integrity and strength. You would only be capable of these things if you could remember that he is a person, if, in fact, he has failed to treat you as one.

In recent months I have heard various Israeli and Palestinian leaders speak. Each of them told of the unreasonable actions taken by the other side. None acknowledged their own side's unreasonable acts. No representative of either side had any problem telling people on the other side what they should do.

Israeli and Palestinian leaders do not have a monopoly on this behavior. We all have a tendency to resist the reality of others, to be focused only on our own needs, and to be caught up in self-justifying images. I am sure that that Israeli official has a family and friends that he cares about deeply. He probably knows how to be responsive to their needs and concerns. Palestinians, for him, are a different reality— a different context. Breaking context would begin by acknowledging that Palestinians are real people. They have needs and concerns. Their needs and concerns are as important to them as his are to him.

Imagine the Israeli government being deeply concerned about the well-being of the Palestinian people. Imagine them making decisions and taking action from this context. What would be the result? Imagine a unified Palestinian government taking a strong stance for peace and refusing to support the violence. What would be the result?

Of course, suicide bombers, violent rhetoric, and threats against Israeli citizens by Palestinians and their supporters do not encourage this context for the Israeli leaders. Neither do bombing or invading Palestinian neighborhoods encourage a stance for peace. This unfortunate and painful situation cannot be blamed on any one group. Like most, if not all conflicts, it continues to exist by collusion, because both sides work together to maintain discord.

Palestinian fighters need for the Israeli government to be insensitive, even cruel. For them, this justifies the violence they create. The Israeli government needs the Palestinians to react with violence, because it justifies the harsh measures they enact. Both sides *need* their own people to continue to suffer to justify their behavior. This is collusion. If you have a strong affection for one side or the other in this conflict, it may be difficult to see this. It is true that both sides have been seriously wronged many times. It is also true that this conflict will continue until the blaming stops. Neither side is going to just go away. Neither will back down from their needs. This conflict continues because both sides support it. This is not to say that each side doesn't wish for peace. Rather, the emotional need for the enemy to be wrong, bad, or deserving of punishment contradicts any peaceful intentions. Each side justifies and provokes the other. Palestinian suicide bombers provoke tougher security measures. Tougher security measures provoke a feeling of being oppressed, which leads to the use of more suicide bombers.

I use international examples for two reasons: first, most of us have heard of the situations so you know what I am talking about. Second, Universal Truths are the same whether you are talking about a war between two nationalities or a war between two cubicles in an office. Conflict offers the illusion that one side is completely to blame and the other is innocent. If this is your context, and you are the "innocent" one, then you are powerless to resolve it in a peaceful manner.

For the realists who may be reading this with a bit of cynicism, in no way is it being suggested that all you have to do is be nice and everything will work out fine. We are talking about a mindset that eliminates blaming. From this mindset we influence others and create new possibilities. In the blaming mode we find ourselves in a place of few possibilities outside of the use of force. The use of force creates counterforce. This is rationalized by an "ends justifies the means" philosophy. Ends and means are the same. We reap what we sow. If it takes force to achieve a goal, you will undoubtedly need force to maintain it.

Realistically, the world is not going to stop blaming or using force today. However, an understanding of the futility and ineffectiveness of blaming opens us to new options. It changes the dynamics in any adversarial relationship. When we let go of our need for the other side to be bad or evil, and focus on resolving the issue, we cannot help but influence them. We move from collusion toward collaboration—working together toward a resolution that works best for all.

In the example of the noisy neighbors earlier, if I am the neighbor who wants peace and quiet, eventually, I will expect you to make noise and disturb me every day. I will experience a rush and feeling of satisfaction when I hear any noise at all coming from your home. In a way, I would be greatly disappointed if you were to stop making noise. Your loudness justifies my anger, my negative opinions and my blaming actions. Your disrespect, in my mind, makes it okay for me to think and say negative things about you. Emotionally, I need you to disrupt my day. You need me to be indignant. This justifies your behavior. Our aggression toward each other maintains our conflict. This is collusion.

Collusion is one of the major ways that we deceive ourselves. We may cast ourselves as innocent victims. We may say that we don't want someone else to behave the way he does. The truth is, we need him to behave the way he does. If we tell ourselves, and whoever will listen, what a jerk he is, what will we say if he suddenly becomes respectful?

We see collusion in workplace conflicts all the time. Where there are management and union conflicts, we see collusion. In adversarial union-management relationships, the union needs for management to be unfair and uncaring toward workers. This way of being justifies their existence. It justifies aggressive union tactics.

Management needs for the union to make unreasonable demands and to protect underperforming workers. It allows management to make excuses for people and production problems. It justifies laying off shifts and closing down plants. "We might have stayed open if the union had been more cooperative."

Mutual blaming allows us to ignore our own contribution to problems. In adversarial conflicts we need for the other side to be blameworthy. Whenever people in a workplace engage in mutual blaming there is a satisfaction gained in seeing others fail. This takes our focus away from the greater good for the whole organization.

This mutual blaming in organizations is like having competing crews on a seagoing vessel. Imagine one crew enjoying the fact that another crew has a leak in their part of the boat. The crew pointing the finger gets to enjoy being right, seeing the other group being wrong, and feeling like a winner. In reality everyone is a loser. The whole boat is sinking.

In our personal and work relationships we collude to maintain our respective stories. A manager's story is that she is a capable manager. She sees her employees making repetitive mistakes. She gets angry and talks down to them. They shouldn't be making these mistakes again. Why not? (because she is a capable manager). Their stories have to do with being smart enough to do this job. She shouldn't be talking down to us (because we are smart and don't deserve it).

As the manager impatiently explains what needs to be done, the employees are focused on how they believe they are being treated. Are they going to get it right next time? Are they motivated to get it right? She sees them as not working smart, as needing to be set straight. They see her as difficult and arrogant. They maintain their respective views of each other by expecting each other to be difficult. The employees' perceived "stupidity" justifies the manager's talking in a demeaning way. The manager's negative and critical way of teaching justifies them not getting it right. They provoke each other.

We stop provoking each other by breaking context. The manager questions her irritation and sees that her story, her image of being capable, is not helping her succeed. She steps back and asks herself: "What is it like to work for a manager who is critical and demeaning when mistakes are made?" The employees may ask: "What is it like to be the manager of employees who keep making the same mistakes over and over again?" Once one person breaks context and responds to the other, it becomes easier for the other to break their blaming context.

A father criticizes his son for getting low grades. The son feels the father doesn't care about him. The father sees himself as a good father who is just trying to help his son. The son sees himself as a failure who cannot please his father. The father thinks critical thoughts toward his son. The son avoids contact with the father. The son puts in more effort and improves from a D to a C in Math. The father says, "You'll never get anywhere in life if all you are going to get is a C. You have to try harder." The son tells himself "Why bother. Nothing ever satisfies him. I might as well not try."

The father asks himself: "What is it like to be my son? How does he feel being criticized constantly? Does this motivate him to succeed? Am I making this about my image as a father, or about his well-being?" In asking these questions the father begins to see his son as a real person. His concern shifts to his son's needs, and not his own. Now he can be truly helpful.

Not all conflicts are adversarial. It is possible to have a difference in opinion and work it out respectfully. People can and do work together to create an agreement that is beneficial to all parties. People do it all the time. There are workplaces where unions sit down with management and work together to create what is best for customers, employees, and the bottom line. This is called principled negotiation. I recommend the book, *Getting To Yes: Negotiating Agreement Without Giving In*. This classic book shows how to negotiate win-win agreements.

The first three steps of this process help people in conflict to respond to each other. Step one is to separate the people from the problem. In this step people are allowed to express their emotions and be heard. There is no need to agree or disagree with the emotions. There is no need to justify the emotions. In listening to people, we validate their emotions. When we validate emotions, we validate the person. Accepting someone's emotions as valid is a way of saying:

"I believe you are important." Usually in conflict we tend to dismiss emotions by ignoring them, criticizing them, or saying they are unreasonable. This practice tends to irritate negative emotions and create resistance. None of us wants to be told we shouldn't be angry when we already are angry.

When we accept the emotions, the reality of another person, we are being responsive. This helps the other person to release the emotion and focus on the issues. Separating the people from the problem helps us to take a calmer look at emotionally charged issues. I volunteered my services as a mediator in a landlord tenant conflict. I called the tenant, who was very upset, and asked her to tell me her story. She talked and I listened, without judging or advising her. She felt much better after talking to me. She had been frustrated that no one would listen to her, and she was afraid of being evicted. I did not solve her problem for her, but my listening helped her to deal with her emotions. She was then more capable of exercising rational judgment. In recognizing, understanding and accepting emotions, we are working with the context of a conflict.

When people are fearful they often don't know what they want. They only know what they don't want. If I am arguing with my wife, I don't want to feel taken advantage of or disrespected. She doesn't want to be ignored or have her feelings dismissed. Once we actually listen to each other and get a handle on the emotions, we can focus on the content of the conflict. We can clarify what each of us really wants.

Step two tells us to focus on interests, not positions. In this step we look at the other person's needs, concerns, and wants. A position is a decision I make on how I can get what I want and need. When people fight over positions it is a win-lose situation. Instead of blaming you for the position you have taken, I can ask you why you have taken it. I can seek to understand your needs and desires. I can explain mine. Once we know what is important to each other, we can move to the next step.

Step three is finding a mutually satisfying solution. We work together to create a solution that we both want. At the very least, we create a solution that we can both live with. Let's take an example how we can move beyond blaming using these three steps.

A few years ago an opportunity arose for my wife to take a part time teaching position at a local college. She had spent the past four years at home with our then four-year-old daughter. I was continuing to work as an independent consultant, coach, and author. She wanted the job. I felt resistant to it, because I knew that a lot more time would be required of me to take care of our daughter. I had already felt I wasn't spending enough time on my work.

I could have felt threatened by this new possibility and blamed my wife. Likewise, she could have seen my resistance as not caring about her needs. She could have thought: "All he thinks about is work." Instead, we both realized the needs of each other and chose to respect them. We listened to each others' concerns. We talked about what our daughter needed.

We did our best to listen to each other without judging. The key was that both of us understood each other. I could understand her desire to spend some time outside the home, to have her own money coming in, and to have her own schedule. She understood my need to write, speak, and secure new business. We focused on our interests. I needed adequate time to write. When she was teaching, there would be times I needed to be with clients. Our daughter needed to be able to go play with friends, but not to be in an institutional setting for long hours.

We worked out a mutually satisfying situation. We wanted each other to have our needs met. She wanted me to write and do what I love. I wanted her to teach and have interests outside the home. Both of us knew that these things would add to our relationship.

When my wife was teaching I spent time with our daughter. I made up the work hours in the evening. If I had a client, we made an arrangement with a woman who did day care in her own home. There were children my daughter's age there. It was like a play date for her. It was a little crazier around our house, but our needs were met.

You may be thinking this is no big deal. Okay, so my wife and I worked out a little problem. Baby-sitting issues are one thing, conflicts that involve large groups are so much more. Certainly there are differences in the levels of complexity, but the principle is the same. If it is our goal to help each other meet our respective needs, and if both sides want a mutually satisfying solution, chances are they will find one. It is when we seek goals that are mutually exclusive that we fail to resolve issues. It is when "my needs" become the only important outcome that we prolong conflict. We justify our position and behavior by saying the other side is "bad" or "wrong" or "evil". Whether you are in conflict with your spouse or with a manager at work, you still have the same decisions to make:

- Do I want to be right or do I want to solve the problem?
- Will I continue to ignore the needs and concerns of the other side, or will I listen deeply to their concerns?
- Will I seek to know their interests or will I just push for my own interests?

As you can see, conflict can be productive or destructive. It is often destructive because we don't separate the people from the problem. This happens because we are too wrapped up in our own needs and fears. Destructive conflict is characterized by blaming. Constructive conflict is characterized by mutual acceptance and respect, deep listening, and a desire to create a win-win situation.

Conflict is a reality of life. Dealing with differences up front and with the intention for mutual well-being is not adversarial. In principled negotiating all parties have the goal of creating a mutually-satisfying agreement. Your well-being is as important to me as my well-being is to me. In any workplace, mutual well-being is important to everyone. If any part of the organization fails, it is a failure of the whole organization. If any part succeeds, it is a success for the whole organization. If I am only out for my department my attitude and action will cause harm to other departments. The harm I cause can affect productivity, quality, morale, profit, customer service, and the livelihood of others.

We all have an instinct for creating a win-win outcome with others. Our understanding of win-win principles gets lost when our emotions take over. We are caught up in our anger and all we want is to be right or to make "them" wrong. Practicing emotional awareness will lift us out of blaming and into a more powerful state.

Summary: Whenever we are in an emotional conflict we are in it together. Our need for each other to be wrong or bad has us maintaining the conflict. This is collusion. Our ability to collaborate on a mutually beneficial solution has us resolving it.

10 Emotional Awareness

Emotional awareness is the key to freeing yourself from the restrictions made by blaming. Emotion is energy. It can be both constructive and destructive. A passion for the possible drove both Gandhi and Hitler. Gandhi's passion for peace and independence helped free his country from the yoke of British colonialism. Hitler's passion for German dominance inspired hatred and violence. It is important that we learn how it is that we create our emotions, and how those emotions impact our decisions and behaviors. Emotion by itself is neither good nor bad. It is what we do with it that matters.

Most people tend to underestimate the importance of emotion. People joke about feelings and avoid talking about them. Our feelings, however, have more power over us than we realize. Emotion runs the stock market. Fear drives people to sell. Feeling confident tends to encourage people to buy. How you feel about someone often determines if you will follow him, vote for him, hire him, buy products from him, sell to him, cooperate, compete, trust or not trust him. Emotion often determines these things outside of any reasoning, or sometimes, in defiance of any reasoning. Emotion sets the tone in relationships. The emotional tone of a manager affects the whole department.

What is emotion? Emotion is your body's response to your thinking. It lets you know how you are doing. When you are listening to intuition and following it, you feel good. When you betray yourself, you feel bad. When you are acting in alignment with what you want, you feel good. When you are off track from what you want, you feel bad.

Emotion provides immediate feedback. Does the emotion ever lie to us? The emotion doesn't lie, but we lie to ourselves about what is causing the emotion. We misinterpret emotion to mean that someone or something is to blame. I worked with an executive director who was highly intelligent and a great visionary. Yet, when one of her staff disagreed with her, or called attention to a contradiction, she felt threatened. Consequently staff members would receive the silent treatment, or in some cases, disciplinary action.

How you see the world interacts with how the world appears to be, and you have an emotional response. If you believe disagreement is disloyalty, then someone's view about your decision is hurtful. No one likes feeling pain, so perhaps you learn how to shift it into anger. Anger feels better, at least for the moment. The anger drives you to react in a way that helps you to regain the illusion of control. The anger, if uncontrolled, becomes destructive, or can even lead to violence. In the case of this director, it led to firings, disciplines, and unionization of her workplace. Intellectually she understood that she created her own emotions, but when threatened, she was unaware that she was creating her own emotion. In her view, it was always them. Her strength, the ability to envision with great emotion, was turned into a weakness as she envisioned herself as victimized by others.

If you know that your emotion comes from your context; if you know that you are creating your own experience; and if you know that you can step outside of yourself, then you have significant emotional awareness. Say that someone criticizes your decision or calls you on a contradiction. You may feel hurt and angry, and lash back. They walk away, but you are still fuming. This time though, you catch yourself being angry and blaming. You acknowledge your anger and your hurt. Maybe you take a walk or do something physical to help you to release the tension. Once things have cooled down, you can acknowledge that you are creating this emotion with your thoughts. What are your thoughts? "Who is he to criticize me? I made the best decision I could." This is blaming and self-justification. By recognizing what you are doing, it's possible to restore yourself to sanity. Being more sane, your thoughts move in a more productive direction. What are the facts? Could it be that the decision was not the best? Did my decision contradict my earlier decisions? Is something else bothering me that contributed to my defensive reaction?

Let's say you sort out the facts. You're still not seeing what he is seeing. You go to see him. "Hey, do you have a minute? You said my decision caused problems and contradicted earlier decisions. I reacted to you and didn't listen very well. I thought about it but I'm not seeing it. I'd like to hear your reasoning." He tells you, and you listen fully. You see the problem. "Thanks for telling me. By the way, I felt pretty defensive when you brought that up. I'm sorry I lashed out at you."

You cannot stop yourself from having an emotion. You can try to suppress it, but it is still there. You can train yourself over time to feel no emotion, and this will take you out of touch with yourself and others. Unemotional people do not bond well with others.

When emotions arise, you have several options.

1. Be aware of how you see the world. Find those perceptions you have that cause negative reactions. Change the perception. For example, I used to react angrily to people who cut me off in traffic. Now I get a handle on it quickly or don't react at all. I perceived their actions as unfair and inconsiderate. I came to realize that people's actions in traffic were not about me at all. They were in a hurry, not paying attention, distracted, daydreaming, or talking to others in their car. It's not up to me to judge them. It is my job to stay safe.

My most important goal is to arrive safely with my passengers. My second priority is to be on time. Getting angry does not help me stay safe. In fact, it puts me and others at risk if I express that anger to another driver. I also realize that sometimes I'm the one who cuts people off—although not intentionally. Sometimes people are in a hurry, and maybe they have good reason. Now I tell myself it's okay. They probably need to get somewhere fast. If someone is really reckless and a danger to all of us, I can call 911 with my cell phone and report the license plate number.

2. You can make a decision not to go there. For example, I used to be a jealous person. My jealousy came from my suspicious and dramatic thoughts. It caused problems for me. When you imagine terrible things your body believes them. You put yourself in a state that seems as if the terrible thing is actually happening. At one point I became tired of doing this to myself and my partner. In this case no trust was being violated. If it had been, I would have had another decision to make—(Do I stay with this person or not? Under what conditions?) I saw how destructive my jealousy was and I made a life changing decision. The decision was to not entertain jealous thoughts and fantasies any more. The next time I was tempted to create jealous fantasies I firmly stated to myself that I wasn't going there. I moved my thoughts to another, healthier topic. I have not had a problem with feeling jealous since the moment of that decision.

3. You can postpone action. If you are totally overwhelmed with emotion, you can take a break. Most of us do not make good decisions when we are in the midst of anger or hurt. When we find ourselves in an emotional state we can decide not to decide anything. Find a way to delay decision making. If appropriate, say how you are feeling, and tell the other person you need time to collect yourself.

4. Face the emotion. This is one way to collect yourself. No one enjoys feeling excessive fear or hurt in their bodies. It is the tendency in our world to cover up emotion. We eat, smoke a cigarette, take a drink, or drug ourselves to escape the unpleasant feelings. Instead of resisting and escaping the feelings, feel them. Sit still, and if you can't do that, walk. Allow yourself to feel the emotion in your body. Stop thinking about what troubles you and place all of your thoughts on your physical feelings. Notice areas of your body that are tense. As you take note and think about the physical feelings, breathe deeply. Breathe by taking the air in and all the way down to your diaphragm. Push your stomach out a little on the in breath. Pull it in a little on the out breath. Breathe and feel the physical symptoms.

Two things will happen. First, the physical discomfort will be relieved. Usually these painful or uncomfortable feelings continue because we feed them with our worrisome, negative, or angry thoughts. By just allowing yourself to feel without the thoughts, the feelings will subside. Second, you find out that you can move through unpleasant emotions and reach a state of calm. Through practice you will become skilled at this. Just breathe and focus on the physical symptoms.

The "normal" thing people do when they experience uncomfortable emotions is to look outside themselves. We blame others and expect them to make us feel better. We expect them to change for us. This expectation is usually unrealistic and unattainable. The only place where we have any real control is within ourselves.

5. Manage externals that tend to be catalysts for stress. If you have tendencies to be late, be unprepared, lose things, be excessively disorganized or forget things, make a decision to change what you do. These poor habits are fuel for self-blaming. Decide what is important and do it. If you have any of these tendencies, what impact do these tendencies have on your relationships, your work, or your ability to succeed? What prevents you from allowing the time needed to prepare or organize? Blaming yourself is unproductive and painful. You only have two real choices: either change what you do, or accept yourself exactly as you are.

6. Whenever you are in situations where you find yourself blaming or complaining, stop. Get clear on what you want. Focus your thinking on what you want to create, not on what you have already created. Take your focus off the problem and place it on the solution.

Emotion is expressed through body language, voice tone, and the words we choose. If we are emotionally unaware, then we find ourselves speaking abruptly, whining, venting, yelling, frowning, smirking, tensing, or slouching without understanding the effect our behavior has on ourselves or others.

When we are able to acknowledge and understand our emotions we can use this ability to change our response. This is called emotional intelligence. It is also called wisdom.

I coached a manager (Brenda) who was having difficulty with a supervisor (Greg) who reported to her. Greg tended to make decisions that were outside of his realm of authority. This caused problems for Brenda as she had to justify spending and other decisions made in her department. Employees reported to me that Brenda and Greg were not getting along well. There had been incidents where Brenda was very abrupt with Greg and his team and where Brenda had departed mumbling under her breath. Greg expressed concerns about Brenda's behavior to the vice president who oversaw Brenda's department. Hence, I was asked to help.

Brenda and I talked about the situation.

Bill: How do you feel when you are around Greg?

Brenda: Well, I feel sort of uncomfortable.

Bill: What do you mean by uncomfortable? Is there tension or discomfort in a particular part of your body?

Brenda: Yes, all over, but especially in my stomach area. I just tense up when I am around him.

Bill: How does that feeling influence your behavior? In other words, do you avoid Greg? Do you choose your words carefully? Do you become frustrated, save it up, and then let it fly?

Brenda: I do avoid him. And when we do speak I do choose my words carefully. And, yes, I think I have let my frustrations get the best of me on a few occasions.

Bill: Let's talk about choosing your words carefully. Do you think you might sound a bit tentative to Greg when you do that?

Brenda: I suppose so.

Bill: Let's look at this from Greg's perspective. I'm Greg. You approach me and I receive your words as tentative—not firm, probably not clear. Do you think I would see you as someone who means what she says, as someone who knows what she is talking about?

Brenda: Probably not. You might see me as weak.

Bill: You are being weak. Your tentative manner tells Greg

you are weak and it makes you feel weak. You send that same ineffective message to yourself. Do you feel like you are being yourself with Greg?

Brenda: Definitely not.

Bill: You are correct, because Brenda isn't weak. But this person you are being with Greg is weak. Tell me how you would like to be when you interact with Greg.

Brenda: Strong, confident, clear—myself.

Bill: That's good. Do you know how to be strong and confident?

Brenda: Yes, I do.

Bill: Show me.

Brenda: What?

Bill: Show me. How would you sit in that chair if you were strong and confident? What would your voice sound like? Who would you be?

Brenda: (Sitting up straighter and speaking clearly.) I'd be just like this. I'd be relaxed.

Bill: Can you feel the difference?

Brenda: Definitely.

Bill: The important thing is to be aware of your emotions. When you feel that tension in your stomach, you know something is up. You feel threatened. That's when you step outside yourself and observe yourself non-judgmentally. You are the owner of your emotions. Don't blame Greg and don't even blame yourself. Accept your emotions, breathe, and let them go. Remind yourself of how you intend to feel (strong and confident) and do what you just did—straighten up, speak confidently and be yourself. You may want to have a talk with Greg.

Brenda: I will do that.

Brenda did have her talk with Greg and communications and expectations were established. She feels much more comfortable now and does not avoid Greg.

Brenda is developing the skill of being able to step outside of herself and observe her emotions. This is difficult for most of us. The real barrier is being caught up in ourselves. We do what we think we need to protect ourselves. For most of us that means keeping quiet and then complaining later. For some, it means attacking someone, putting him on the defensive. Once you take charge of your emotions, you have to ask yourself: "What do I want to come of this?" Clarify what would be in the best interest of all concerned and respond to the appropriate person.

Emotional awareness is difficult. Most of the people in the world don't have it. People are driven by blaming, hatred, resentment, bitterness, and fear. Instead of blindly pushing ourselves into conflict and trouble, we have a choice. We can stop and look at the emotion, and ask: "What is this about? How are my actions affecting others? What future impact might they have? Am I thinking clearly enough to know what I want? If so, what do I really want?"

These questions help us to create emotional health. Instead of allowing negative thoughts and emotions to run amok, we can step outside of ourselves and observe. We can make a decision as to what to do with these emotions. We can decide whether or not to pursue these thoughts. We will notice that in most cases we are not so much being attacked by the words of others, but by our own thoughts. We can call off the attack. We can decide to think about something else, or to perceive the person or situation differently. Through practice we find that we can control and channel emotion in constructive ways.

Emotion is energy. We can let it destroy us, or we can focus it on a passion for something joyful. We do this by shifting our attention from that which we don't want to that which we do want. We can shift our attention from anger at having no money to a passion for being prosperous. We can shift our stress and frustration with co-workers to a passion for teamwork. We can shift from resentment for being ill to a passion for being well. Whenever you find yourself caught up in negative emotion ask: "What do I want to come of this? What do I want instead?" Shift your energy toward your passion and your vision for what can be.

Emotional awareness helps us to understand that we are not our emotions. We experience emotions. As an observer of your own experience you are capable of making emotionally intelligent decisions.

This is not suppression of emotion. You can feel an emotion and accept it without allowing it to drive your behavior. You can express the emotion of your body guided by the wisdom of your mind. As you move beyond blaming and take full ownership of the emotions you create, you become more adept at utilizing emotion to achieve what you really want.

Summary: Emotional awareness is the key to moving beyond blaming. Our ability to notice, address, and refocus negative emotion frees us from being a victim or an attacker. It provides us with the ability to create peace and health in our own minds, in our relationships, and in our organizations.

11 Clarity

We blame and complain, but most of us don't know what we want. The next time you hear yourself blaming and complaining, ask yourself what you really want. What do you want the situation to be? You might say: "I want that person to stop doing that thing that they are doing." Having said that, you have just stated what you don't want. Thinking more deeply, you respond: "I want to be treated with respect." What would that look like and feel like? What would you need to do to encourage respect?

Once you know what you want, you have created an intention. An intention is an aim, a destination, a desired situation. Intentions are powerful, because they focus your thoughts and emotions on what you want. Your focus opens your mind to new ideas. You become especially alert. Many years ago I created the intention that I wanted a new car— a Ford Taurus. I started seeing Taurus's everywhere. There may have been just as many Honda Accords or Pontiac Grand Ams out on the roads, but it seemed like there were more Taurus's. There were plenty available for sale, so it didn't take long to find one at the price I was willing to pay. Once you are clear about what you want, with no doubt, your mind automatically becomes alert to the possibilities for making it happen.

If you are blaming another person for issues in your relationship, all you will see is blame. You will focus on what is wrong with the other person. Your intention, then, is to prove the other person wrong and you right. Your innocence and the other person's guilt become your goal. At the same time, you may be saying that you want to make this relationship work. You want to get along, to work well together, to be friends, or to be loving, depending on the type of relationship it is. Now you have two conflicting intentions. One moment you are thinking, speaking, and acting in ways that encourage a positive relationship. The next moment you are thinking, speaking, and acting in ways that blame, condemn, attack, and defend.

When you are blaming, the other person is an object. You cannot have a positive relationship with an object. You must remind yourself that this person is real. A positive relationship requires mutual respect and understanding. It requires that you see the other person clearly. If you are blaming, you are trapped in your own issues and concerns. Step out of your concerns and into the world. Listen to the other person with the intent to understand.

Here is where the intention to blame kicks in. I say: "Understand how the other person feels." You react: "Why should I listen to her? She doesn't listen to me. Why should I care? She doesn't care." It is at this point that you must decide on your intention. What do you want? Do you want to be "right" or do you want to resolve issues and create a positive relationship? You cannot have both. Being right is irrelevant to a positive relationship.

By now you may be asking: "How do I resolve issues if the other person insists on being right?" You make your intentions clear, and you ask the other person what they intend. They may tell you what they don't want. Listen and understand clearly what they don't want. Then ask them what they do want. People who are stuck in the blaming mode are focused on what they don't want. They believe that if they could just get rid of what they don't want, everything would be okay. Ask people what they want. Help them to clarify what they want. This gives them something to shoot for rather than someone to shoot at.

Whenever I work with people in conflict, I always ask them what they want. It gets them to look at where they are focusing their energy. It helps to refocus their energy toward their possibilities. Whenever I am in conflict, I ask myself: "What do I want to come of this?"

I had a business partner who had a habit of showing up late for meetings. I was not only irritated, but embarrassed. It made our partnership look unprofessional to our client. In the blaming mode I could criticize him for being late and tell him he had better get there on time. If I were more passive I might keep it to myself and let my criticism and anger simmer below the surface. I might entertain thoughts of dissolving the partnership, telling him off, or finding a new partner. If my thoughts head in this direction, what is my intention? I might say it is for him to be on time. This would not be honest. My emotional energy tells me my real intention.

My energy is flowing toward criticism, frustration, and ending the relationship. Maybe I should end the relationship. The question still stands before me: "What do I want?" I breathe deeply and let go of the stress. I ask myself what I want and I write it down. I want a professional partnership based on trust and competency. I want to know my partner is going to be on time and be prepared. I want to be seen by clients as a strong, competent team that can address their needs with sensitivity and expertise.

Now that I know my intention I can approach my partner. "You've been late the last two meetings. What's going on?"

He responds, "I just didn't allow myself enough time. It took longer than I thought to get there."

"When either of us is late, it makes us look bad to the client. I try to cover for you and make the client feel comfortable. This isn't what I envisioned when we started partnering. My vision is this: I want a professional partnership where we are both on time and well-prepared. I see us delivering a high-end service that inspires our clients' trust and confidence in us. What do you think?"

"Sounds good to me."

"Can I count on you to be on time for meetings?"

"I'll try."

"What do you want out of this?"

"I want to do business with a lot of clients and make a lot of money."

"Are you committed to that? Are you willing to do what it takes to grow this business?"

"Yeah, I am."

"Are you willing to show up on time and prepared?"

"I'll try."

"Telling me you will try to be on time doesn't sound like a commitment. It's great to make a lot of money, and the way to do that is to offer a highly professional and valuable service. If people can't trust us to do what we say we're going to do, then we aren't going to succeed."

"You know, I just have this issue with being on time. I will try. I promise."

"Being late is not an issue; it's a decision. You know when the meeting starts, you plan accordingly, and you allow enough time to get there. Obviously, emergencies happen. If something happens you call ahead and let people know. All of this is decision making. I'm asking you to make a decision that you will be on time. Either you are willing to make this kind of decision or you aren't.".

My intention is clear. The approach is direct and honest. I'm not saying he should be on time. The choice is his. I am not willing to maintain a business relationship where I cannot trust my partner to be there. Relationships need to be flexible, yet we need to identify clear boundaries. If we allow others to cross those boundaries we commit an act of self-betrayal. As we have already explained, self-betrayal leads to self-portrayal, self-justification, and blaming. We can eliminate much of this by being clear.

In my experience, most leaders are not clear about their expectations. They want people to do things, blame them when they don't, and struggle with the results. Leaders must clarify what they want. What would it look like, feel like, and be like? Every leader is a vision holder who must keep the vision in front of the people. This involves continuous feedback to people on their work, their behavior, and their accomplishments. It involves timely feedback when people are not in alignment with the vision. If you ignore people who behave in ways that contradict the vision, then you are giving your permission. Your intention has shifted from achieving the vision to avoiding conflict, playing it safe, or saving time.

Blaming and complaining about people who are not performing, not following the rules, or producing poor quality work is useless. Teach people your vision. Criticism keeps people focused on what you don't want. Show people what can be, and show them how they can get there. Treat them with the kind of respect that envisions them already being there. In other words, to have a world-class work place, treat your employees as if they are already world-class. Offer that level of respect and attention. Every employee is a world-class worker in training.

The same concept can be applied to your family. If you want mature, responsible children, treat them as if they already are. Don't blame them when they falter. Take responsibility. Respond to them. Find out who they are; don't resist who they are. This is really tough, because we parents always want to give advice. We get offended when our children don't want to take it. Focus on their needs as children, not on your needs as a parent. My need to look good as a parent is secondary to being fully present for them. It should not be their burden to make me look good. It's not about me fixing them with parental platitudes. Fortunately for me, I have two grown-up children who let me know when I'm not listening. I am grateful for that.

Once, my youngest daughter screamed and cried in the grocery store because I wouldn't let her have candy. I held her close and gently, yet firmly explained why she couldn't have it. I don't know if the several people standing nearby thought I was a good parent or not. It doesn't matter. Three year olds sometimes scream and cry when they don't get what they want. I did the most loving thing I could at the moment. I listened; I offered my concern; I empathized; and I made my intention clear (no candy). The next time we went to the store she went after the same candy. I said she couldn't have it. She said okay and put it down.

Clarity and responsiveness are a powerful combination. When you are clear about what you want, and you are responsive to the person you are talking to, people notice. People begin to respond to you. Your clarity and responsiveness build trust and respect. Your boundaries become clear and people respect them. As a leader, whether at home or work, you respect the boundaries of others, too.

We often expect people to know our boundaries and expectations. They usually don't know them unless we communicate. Poor performance, low productivity, inconsistency, and unprofessional behavior all come from a lack of clear expectations. The leadership in any organization that is struggling with people issues needs to ask itself: "What do we want?"

Organizations may appear to be thriving, but ask the people who work there how they feel. If there is no vision; if leadership is not responsive to people; the organization is dying. You don't have to go out of business to die. If people lack motivation; if work is seen as drudgery; if relationships are stressed; if people can't wait to get out of there — it's dying. Some organizations are perpetually dying.

Clarity and responsiveness will bring resurrection. Create a vision and enroll people in it. Ask for their input on how to achieve the vision. Ask them what they need to make it happen at their level. Educate them on the importance of their role and the impact of their actions on others. Offer continuous positive feedback on their performance. Immediately take corrective action (responsively without blaming) when people are off track. Listen to people.

When you are clear things start to change. If you want to change your organization, get clear on what you want. If you want to change your life, get clear on what you want. Get clear on how you want to feel. Commit yourself to your vision. A vision is not about the future. It is about now. It doesn't come someday. You begin your vision right now by thinking and feeling as if it has already arrived.

Summary: Once you are clear about what you want and who you are your power grows. Your intent focuses your thoughts, emotions, words and behaviors. Clarity means that you not only strive for what you want; you become what you want.

12 Unleashing Your Power

We all have power. The question for each of us is: How are we using it? Oddly enough, most of us use our power to make ourselves powerless. Blaming is a way of pretending we are not powerful. In blaming we pretend that we can only be successful, or that things will be better, if someone or something outside of our control changes. When we blame ourselves, we focus our energy on being helpless or unworthy. Helplessness and unworthiness become our entire image of ourselves, and influence all of our behavior. Encouraging shame and guilt in ourselves, and in others, disempowers us.

When we are blaming, our vision is one of being right and finding fault. This becomes our intention. Yet, most people when asked, would say that their intention is to create success. The teacher who criticizes the underperforming student in front of the whole class believes that she is helping the student to succeed. In most cases, she isn't. The goal of public criticism is submission. Does she want the student to submit to her opinion, or does she want him to be empowered to stretch and learn?

The same could be said about managers who constantly criticize certain employees. Criticism usually doesn't motivate employees. Do we want submissive employees who do what they are told, or do we want empowered employees who know what to do and who take responsibility for their work? If you want the latter, criticism will not get you there. The critical approach creates frustration both for you and the person you criticize.

I once worked with a CEO who was constantly frustrated with one of his senior managers. His approach was to criticize. The manager was always on the defense, making excuses, and avoiding responsibility. I asked them to meet at a job site. I asked the CEO to clarify his priorities and expectations for the manager. He specifically outlined what he wanted, his vision, and his priorities. The manager told me it was the first time he had heard that information in twenty years.

The CEO would tell the manager what to do without offering him a complete vision of what was to be. When the manager made mistakes, the CEO aggressively criticized him. The manager spent his energy explaining his reasons for making certain choices or mistakes rather than on getting a clear vision of what he needed to do. It was a game of cat and mouse that went on for years.

The CEO had not communicated his vision very well. The manager had not asked what the vision was. There was constant guessing and second guessing. Neither of them were willing to give up the game of mutual blaming, although both would tell you it was the other who refused to change.

Clear vision and expectations make us more powerful, yet we must go deeper than words. We can communicate our vision and expectations to others and still be frustrated with the results. We can do all the right things on the surface and still fail.

If we are doing the right things, but doing them from a mindset of blaming, we will most likely produce frustration for ourselves. We may get excellent work products or services, but we will have to be on people constantly to get things done. The blaming mindset needs to be changed. Each of us needs to ask ourselves: "Who am I being? What am I creating?" A reflective leader will ask himself: "Is what I'm doing effective? Am I getting the results I want?" The deeper more essential question is: "Is who I'm being bringing me the results I envision?" Power comes from focusing on what we are giving out to others and ourselves. Powerlessness comes from focusing on what we are or are not getting from others.

In the example of the CEO and the manager, neither was willing to consider what he was contributing to the situation. There was the assumption that one's own attitude and behavior was correct. The problem was with the other person. In this particular relationship, the CEO couldn't fathom what it was like for the manager to work for a critical, uncommunicative boss. The manager couldn't understand what it was like for the CEO to have a manager who often did not make sound decisions or follow through. Power was there to be gained through a mutual understanding of each other and their vision, but both focused on what they thought they were getting from the other.

We create our own experience. Meg is a department manager at a small, family-owned company that is having difficulties. Based on her experiences dealing directly with clients, she has developed some good ideas for turning things around. The family that runs the company is pretty unreceptive to ideas from those outside of their clique. Meg goes home every night fearing that the company may fail, and that she may lose her job. She's sure she knows how to fix things, but is extremely frustrated that none of her ideas are ever implemented. The more she thinks about it, the more the management clique seems lazy, selfish, and ignorant.

She feels forced to keep doing her job in a way that she knows is simply not working. More and more, her days at work are spent resenting the company owners. On one hand, she understands how things are. On the other hand, she sees how she wants them to be. This gap between how she sees it and how she wants it is her frustration. Her frustration is that management won't let her do what she wants. She believes her ideas would make the organization better. She feels powerless. She complains that she works with unintelligent people. They can't see the wisdom of her ideas. They don't get it.

Meg's focus in this example is on what she thinks everyone else is doing to her. In her mind, they are stopping her from succeeding. She is not seeing what she is doing to everyone else. If you were to ask her what she was doing for the organization, she would tell you she was giving her best, and working hard. This is probably true, yet who is she being behind all of this hard work? What kind of person is she being?

If you are a joyful person in your thoughts, you offer joy to the organization. If you are focused on what is highest and best for the organization, you offer what is highest and best. If you are frustrated and blaming, what do you offer the organization? Your thoughts, and the feelings around them, are what you are offering. You offer what is in you. I offer what is in me. We receive back what we offer. In other words, if we offer irritation, we're going to receive more irritation. We get what we are giving. We tell ourselves that others are giving us irritation, but we are giving it to ourselves. We each create our own experience.

If Meg spends a lot of time blaming and complaining about other people or about how things are, she can be assured of only one thing – she is probably a major pain to at least some of the people around her, regardless of how valid or right her complaint might be. Whatever dissatisfaction is bubbling up within her is the gift that she gives to everyone who is around her. No matter whether her ideas are implemented or not, she is always contributing her attitude to the group. If it is her vision to have a high-performing workplace, or harmonious relationships, she needs to see each and every person as an important part of this vision. When she is able to view others in this way, then she can play a major role in leading them into this vision. Complaining or feeling righteous has no positive effect.

Actions inspired by negativity usually create a negative effect. Actions inspired by something positive usually create a positive effect. Let's say Meg hears this advice and decides to be positive. She starts praising the people around her. If she believes that they are lazy, selfish, and ignorant, her praise may actually have a negative effect. She will tell herself that she tried to be positive but it didn't work. It is true that her words were positive, but the person she was being behind those words was not positive. She was using "positive" behaviors in order to get others to change. Her newfound and short-lived positive behavior sets her up to confirm her belief – management is lazy, selfish, and ignorant.

Their negative response is a reflection of her negative assumptions about them. She doesn't really respect them or believe in them, and they can feel it. It doesn't matter what she says. What matters is how she feels toward them. More than her good ideas, what she thinks and feels is what she is offering them.

This principle is true in any relationship. If I think my wife is an incredible woman, my compliments to her will be taken appreciatively. I am giving her what I have — love, appreciation, admiration. If I think she is selfish and undeserving, and I give her a compliment, my compliment will not be fully appreciated. Despite what I am saying, I am still giving her what I have — my negative perception.

When people say they are trying to get along it is often not true. Trying to get along while still spending all your energy focusing on someone else's wrongness just doesn't work. At best, you create a truce. At worst, you become more angry and justify more acts of aggression. Power is found in changing your assumptions. The diagram in Chapter Five demonstrates how assumptions lead to self-protective behaviors. The only way out of the vicious cycle of blaming is to challenge your assumptions. This is true of any relationship or situation.

When people are dealing with a problem situation the tendency is to come up with reasons. Reasons are not necessarily causes. Reasons are usually justifications based on the assumption that we are powerless to affect the true cause. If my reason for slow business is the economy, I know that I cannot change the economy. What I can change is my assumption that a poor economy automatically means my income will be limited. I need to take my mind off the poor economy and focus on what I want to create.

We are constantly frustrated in relationships and in organizations because we are unaware of how we affect others. The reasons we give for things not going well are part of the cause. Look at any relationship or situation. What are you giving to it? What you are giving to it is how you are affecting it. This is how you are powerful. The situation that frustrates you, the person who irritates you, the people who won't listen to you— are all results you are producing. You become more powerful when you take your mind off what you think people and situations are doing to you. Place your mind, instead, on the positives that you want to create. Focus on what you want and respond to people and situations that are in front of you.

This shift in your attention often begins with dissatisfaction. We find ourselves feeling frustrated, angry, intolerant, or unhappy. This initial dissatisfaction is important. It is a place to begin the change process. In this beginning stage we identify what is not working and how we feel about it. Our negative emotion motivates us to do something about the situation. The next step is to identify what we do want. We look for the possibilities and access how we would feel if the possibilities were realized. This positive emotion is what we bring to the change process.

Once you have the awareness that you really can affect your reality, you stop needing for people and situations to change themselves for you. You have removed your focus from that which you can't control to that which you can. As you withdraw your need to affect others, you find that you actually start to have more impact. Your power has increased and this creates greater responsibility for you. The principle is this: It is not how others see you that creates the problem; it is how you see them. If you want to change your relationships, personal or professional, change the way you see those people. Stop criticizing. Start seeing the best in them.

People feel your clarity, your positive expectations, your caring, and your non-attachment to the choices they make.

Blaming is experienced as an attack. Those who are blamed focus their energy on defense and counterattack. When you are no longer attacking they have nothing to defend. This serves to encourage people to look at themselves, to ask themselves what they want. Your obvious support for their well-being facilitates trust in the relationship. They look to you for guidance. Their focus changes from defending themselves to seeking something better for themselves. Of course, there are people who will not respond positively to your shift in being. These people are disappointed that you are no longer attacking. These people who are not ready to change, if allowed to experience their own consequences, will create their own misfortune.

Clarity of vision, clear expectations, understanding of the needs of others, and non-attachment to what others think and do are a powerful combination. This power can be used for the highest good of all, or it can be used to manipulate. This is the difference between a Martin Luther King, Jr., and an Adolph Hitler. King's power was great. Few people can listen to the "I have a dream" speech and not be moved. His power came from his clarity of vision and his passion for the idea that ALL people could live together in peace. Hitler's power appeared to be great, also. Millions were moved by his passionate ideas. His influence was used to unify one group for purposes of destroying other groups. The misuse of power usually turns sour and results in the use of force.

The key difference between the positive use of power and the negative use of power is this: positive power is used to make others powerful. The misuse of power is about making others serve you or your agenda. A manager may be able to provoke his staff into high productivity by manipulating their emotions. He can use potential job loss, loss of status, fear of disapproval, or the need to be liked by him as motivators to get what he wants. Leaders who discover their power but have a personal agenda easily resort to force. They believe that the ends justify the means.

That same manager can utilize power in a very different way. He can use it to make his people powerful. He can use it to help them see their own potential and work to realize it. This is the kind of power we are talking about unleashing. As you unleash this power in yourself, you will find your influence with others growing. What will you do with it? Will you use it to empower them, or will you use it to serve yourself? The temptation to use power for purely selfish ends or to take shortcuts to achieve your agenda is always present. The leader who is conscious of this understands that ends and means are the same. You reap what you sow. The cost of the misuse of power and manipulative leadership is always high.

When people know that you truly care about their interests, you become influential. When people feel that you believe in them, at least a part of them responds with heightened motivation to succeed. There is never anything to justify or defend. There is no one to blame. You know that you are speaking and acting from complete integrity. Integrity gives you strength. You feel good about yourself. People give you their trust. They are happy to help you.

Often I have asked factory workers if they have ever had a great supervisor. Most say that they have. I asked them what made the supervisor great. Answers have been consistent.

"He thanked us for our good work every day."

"He always asked our opinion before making decisions that affected us."

"She listened to us."

Each time I asked: "Would you go the extra mile for that supervisor?" the answer was always in the affirmative. These supervisors had power because people wanted to perform well in the environment created by their supervisor.

It is difficult to establish this power when we are engaged in image management. We worry about how others see us. We are concerned about how we come across, what people think of us, and how we measure up. People around us become our audience. Our focus on a need to fulfill a certain image distances us from others. We invest our energy into trying to control the thoughts and actions of others. Our focus on image management prevents us from seeing what is really happening. We are lost in our own world, so we cannot respond to what is happening in the real world.

Powerful people pay attention to the things others don't. Truly powerful people see that a person is upset, excited, not being truthful, sincere, or troubled. Powerful people are not afraid of emotion in themselves or in others. They accept that people are where they are at a given moment. There is no need to change them. Powerful people are aware of their own thoughts and emotions. It is within themselves where efforts at change are focused.

If you are in integrity with yourself, responsive toward others, and clear about your goals, you find yourself in control of how you communicate. You will speak with authority. People will see you as real. You need not manage your image, only your tendencies to want to impress others.

How do we apply this to the frustrated manager whose superiors won't let her do what she wants? First, she has to stop blaming and complaining. Meg has to stop telling herself that they should be acting any differently than they are. She needs to stop creating an image of unintelligent people. As she begins to release this negativity, she can start to look for positives. What does she appreciate about them? In what ways have they shown themselves to be competent? What good things can she say about them? She needs to develop some positive assumptions about them. She can do this by getting to know them better. She can build stronger relationships. She can envision a strong collaborative relationship with them. She can learn about their needs and desires. What do they care about? When she and they talk, instead of a constant critical monologue running through her mind, she can be fully present and listen to them. Her understanding of their interests will help her to create possibilities that will help all of them succeed. Her supportive attitude will help them to want to listen to her.

Your ability to help someone else depends on your willingness to see them as worthy of your help, rather than worthy of your blame. Your ability to see potential in someone else is power. You can help that person find a pathway to that potential. If you have ever had a teacher, coach, leader, or parent who believed in you more than you believed in yourself, then you have experienced this power. As a result, you came to believe in yourself. You felt encouraged and inspired.

In organizations, families, and relationships, we are in it together. You are connected to everyone else, whether you admire them or blame them. When you are keenly aware of that connection, you recognize that your attitude affects others. Your thoughts about others affect them, and they affect you. You influence others by caring about them, seeing the potential in them, and clearly knowing who you are. If you see others as different than you, less valuable, less important, less worthy, then you are disconnected from them. You cannot influence others positively from a place of disconnection.

You connect by giving others unconditional positive regard. You see the best in them and you keep in mind their innate worthiness. You value them regardless of their looks, performance, or rank. At the same time, you might also value them for those things. In other words, you may value others for their skill or accomplishment, and you will also value them if they don't have that skill or accomplishment.

People who live in a connected world are powerful. The only price for this power is the relinquishment of your victimhood. Your power is unleashed when you begin to question the assumption that anybody is doing anything to you. Your power increases when you recognize that whatever your experience is, you are doing it to yourself. Once you top the crest of that mountain, life flows more easily. Once you feel the power of complete responsibility your passion begins to grow.

You know that the high-performing organization, the harmonious relationship, or the loving family are possible. Your way of being, your passion for the possible, invites others into the vision.

You empower others by believing in their capability to manifest the vision. This belief sparks their passion. If you are believing in the potential of those around you, seeing their best qualities, and doing what is needed to improve situations, you can be assured of one thing — You are probably an inspiration to at least some of the people around you.

The most limiting thought we carry is that others are the leaders, and we are required to follow. Power is unleashed when we realize that we are all leaders. You can lead from where you stand. You lead by creating a vision, a possibility, and giving it your passion. You bring the joy of your vision into all that you say and do. You offer that passion and your belief to others by believing in their possibilities.

Summary: Power is unleashed when we shift our focus from blaming to discovering the possibilities within every person and situation. Power and passion are unleashed when we shift from a focus on what we are getting from a situation to what we are giving to it. Influence with people is increased when we see ourselves as connected to others. We cannot influence from a place of disconnection.

13 The Power of Non-Attachment

It was said earlier that it is important to let go of your need for others to change. This is called non-attachment. The principle of non-attachment has you envisioning success, embarking on the path to success, yet being completely unattached to the results. That is, you don't need those results to feel good about yourself. You want a certain result, but you don't have to have it. Non-attachment makes you powerful. If I must close this sale, the tension I create will most likely interfere with the results I desire. My need affects my potential buyer in a negative way. If the buyer feels my need, he will more than likely hesitate or leave the deal on the table. If my attitude is that I only want this deal if it benefits the buyer, then I am willing to walk away if it doesn't. The buyer feels my willingness to walk away and is influenced by it.

Manipulators use non-attachment as a tactic. They will take the deal away from a prospect with something like: "Maybe this deal isn't for you. It's not right for everyone. Not everyone has the right qualifications." The inexperienced buyer will feel motivated to buy. The experienced buyer will see the game, and it will backfire.

True non-attachment has a similar effect. It makes people want to buy. The difference here is there is no game to expose. The buyer and the seller have the same goal: the deal has to be a win-win, or there won't be a deal. Prospects are more likely to buy because the seller doesn't need them to buy.

The principle of non-attachment is based on the truth that your positive intention will bring you the right results from the right people. There is nothing mystical about this. You always have more power when you can withdraw your need for things to turn out exactly as you think they should turn out. A focus on needing certain results has us trying to control people and things. Trying to control that which we cannot control results in feeling powerless. You win when you become willing to do without the prize.

Your well-being comes from your state of mind. Remember the statement from Chapter Five: "It's your call." It is not what happens to you that makes you happy or unhappy, but the meaning you attach to it. Knowing that your well-being comes from within, you are never a victim. Knowing your well-being comes from within, your power to achieve greatness is unleashed.

I once counseled a fifteen-year-old boy who intended to run away. He thought he would hitchhike across the country, steal a guitar, and start his own band. This was a serious situation and a serious mistake for him to make. Most people's first instinct would be to forbid him from doing this and to try to talk him out of it. In that moment though, I became unattached as to whether he would run or not. I didn't think about what I thought would be the best choice for him. My goal was his well-being. I listened to his ideas and took them seriously. I didn't argue with him. I asked some questions in the spirit of helping him plan his trip. I wanted to make his fantasy real to him so he could make a more informed decision. I asked whether he had ever hitchhiked before, where he would sleep, what he would eat, how he would stay warm, and other practical questions. Of course, he had never given much thought to these questions. He was seeing himself as the successful rock guitarist of his vision. Suddenly the inherent difficulties in his plan became very real. He changed his mind and stopped threatening to run away.

We are most effective with others when we are unattached to their decisions. Non-attachment doesn't mean not caring about the person. It means not assuming we know what is best for someone else. If my employee does poor quality work, I should help him. I offer help, I do what I can to respond to his needs, and I create a structure to help him to succeed. If he can't, or decides he won't improve, I must respond. Either I move him to another job, or if that isn't possible, I help him leave. I don't know what is best for that employee. Protecting him from his own consequences may actually prevent him from learning or finding more appropriate work.

If I become attached to the idea that he must succeed at this job I limit our possibilities. Both of us become more powerful when we become willing to discover what is highest and best for him and for the organization. This opens up a whole world of possibilities. The message of the principle of non-attachment is this: Give up your job as manager of the world. The job is too big for you to handle. Instead take on the job as manager of your thoughts. This will make you powerful.

Summary: We are more likely to find success when we let go of our need to control the results. As we focus on managing our thoughts rather than the behavior of others, we become more powerful.

14 Conversation

It has been said that one of the greatest fears people hold is speaking in front of a group of people, yet we seem to have no shortage of public speakers. There is a kind of speaking that inspires greater fear. This is the fear of having a real conversation.

Sound bites are not conversation. The rantings and ravings of radio talk show hosts are not conversation. Talking about the weather is not conversation. Conversation is when two or more people talk openly and honestly, listen deeply to each other, and reach a common understanding. Agreement is nice, but irrelevant. The art of conversation is not about getting someone to agree with you. It is about seeking and finding a common understanding.

The first goal in conversation is to understand the thinking of the other person. The second goal is to articulate one's own thinking in a way the other can understand. A true conversation is blameless, non-judgmental, direct, and respectful. Conversation is a way of connecting.

Most of us are afraid of a real conversation. If we really listen to someone else, it may upset our world view, our self-image, or our view of life. We might find out we were wrong. We might discover how they really feel about us. If we said what we really felt, the other person might be hurt, angry, disapproving, or judging. They might take action against us.

We are afraid of conflict. It poses a threat. We don't want to be rejected, hurt, or embarrassed. The thought of conflict provokes the flight or fight response. We either avoid or attack when we feel threatened. We do everything but engage in conversation.

In our organizations and families we are starving for conversation. Blaming takes its place. It's easier. It's easier to tell myself how wrong you are than it is to tell you I want to have a conversation. Many will say: "I tried that. I tried talking to that person." Trying to get someone to see it your way is not a conversation. It is certainly important to state your preferences. In conversation you are willing to suspend your judgments and conclusions while you listen to the other person. You are willing to allow new conclusions to arise as products of your mutual understanding.

Conversation is responsive. In it we see the other person as a real person. We accept who they are. We see past perceived differences in gender, race, ethnicity, religion, intelligence, sexual preference, economic status, age, profession, title, or background. They are first, and foremost, a person. You are first, and foremost, a person.

Moving beyond blaming makes it possible to have a conversation. Conversation helps us build a mutual understanding. Occasionally I meet someone I dislike. I purposely initiate a conversation. More often than not, I come away with an appreciation for the person. The dislike I felt was in me, not in them. It was my projection.

It all begins with the "conversation" we are having in our own heads. If your tendency is to be critical toward self and others in your mind, it will manifest in your way of being with others. What do you tell yourself about yourself? What do you tell yourself about others? Constant self-talk in a blaming mode creates a negative emotional state. In a negative emotional state, you are unable to converse. Everything you say will come across as blaming. The impact of your talk will encourage defensiveness.

When you experience negative emotion ask yourself: "What is the impact of this conversation in my mind and how is it affecting me?" Be willing to step outside yourself and notice who you are being. Is this what you want? There have been times I have found my thinking tottering on the lip of insanity, ascribing all sorts of negative motivation to others. I would step back and ask myself: "What are you thinking? This isn't really happening. You're making it up!" Inevitably I would recover my sanity and find my mental musings to be false.

How often do we give ourselves negative messages about others without actually talking to them? How often do our negative thoughts become self-fulfilling prophecies when we treat people as if they have already offended us? How often do we refuse to hear the facts because we already have an opinion?

When you are experiencing difficulty with others ask: "What is the conversation I am having and what impact is this having on this person? How am I allowing them to affect me?" Again, you briefly step outside yourself and observe. Ask yourself if this situation is what you want.

It is certainly okay to express your anger. For example, you could say: "When you did that, I was angry." Conversations are not always perfectly rational. Just remember you are talking to a real person. Conversations need not be devoid of emotion. Emotion adds meaning to conversation. Maintain an awareness of your emotion and the effect it is having on your conversation.

Not all attempts to converse will be welcomed. So what? If someone refuses to move beyond blaming, so what? If someone doesn't want to listen to you, so what? Do it anyway. You have to detach yourself from needing any particular response. Your well-being comes from within you. Joy is a decision. Feeling rejected is a decision. Your mind, your spiritual connection, and your ability to create positive emotion will meet your needs. As you learn to meet your own needs you will find others wanting to help you meet your needs. Your healthy sense of being will draw to you other healthy people. Birds of a feather do fly together.

A lack of communication produces a void. People fill in the void with thoughts that assume blame. Insist on communicating with people. Refuse to blame them when they don't communicate with you. Refuse to be disturbed by the opinions of others. Your ability to listen and to express your truth will be influential. Is there someone you are blaming right now? Consider having a conversation.

Progress is not measured by your ability to convince others. It is measured by your ability to understand one another. Disagreeable people are sandpaper, refining you, smoothing you, and shaping you. Conflict used well, helps you to grow. Welcome disagreement and conflict. Make them your friends. Accept them as part of life.

Let your conversations affirm others. You may see another's argument as false or foolish, yet offer your respect to the person. Your respect will do more to help them see the holes in their logic than a personal attack. It is through affirmative conversation that people are inspired, lifted up, and helped to see new possibilities. Whether you are praising or reprimanding, make your conversation helpful. Make your intent be for the highest good for all concerned. Conversation is powerful. It is your contribution to the well-being of everyone.

Summary: The goal of conversation is mutual understanding. I listen to you. You listen to me. We may or may not agree, but we do understand each other. In conversation we are conscious of the needs and concerns of the other person.

15 Changing A Blaming Culture

This chapter is for leaders, and we are all leaders. It applies to how we think and act in organizations. Typically, most people in organizations tend to think there is little they can do to create positive change. We tolerate negative situations, believing there are few solutions out there. In this we are correct, few solutions are "out there". We have been looking in the wrong places.

Often people operate on automatic pilot in organizational life. We feel compelled to think and act in certain ways and we don't question them. Whatever is happening is seen as reality, and seldom do people understand that they are creating this reality. The tendency is to think reality is happening to us. In Chapter Six, we talked about context. In organizations we have a shared context.

Organizations are driven by thought. How we think determines the assumptions we make. Our assumptions determine our relationship to other people, technology, processes, authority, and the interests we serve. Our assumptions determine the choices we make, and our choices become our structure. Peter Senge in his book, *The Fifth Discipline*, defines structure as "choices made over time." Our choices made over time become the assumed way things are done.

Our thoughts, feelings, assumptions, relationships, and choices become the system. To borrow from Dr. Senge again, ". . . our organizations work the way they work, ultimately, because of how we think and how we interact." Positive change and growth come from a willingness to question how we think and how we interact.

This has been referred to as "thinking out of the box". To me, thinking out of the box means questioning the thinking that goes on beneath our conscious thought process. In my thinking I may say that a certain department is to blame for poor service. There may be some truth here. The department may have problems, but it also operates within, and depends upon, a larger community, which includes me. On what assumption do I base the conclusion that the department is the problem? The willingness to question our assumptions takes us out of the box and into the realm of possibility.

Many organizations have a blaming culture. In these organizations people point the finger, complain, criticize, and make excuses. In a blaming culture time and energy are spent proving someone else is wrong, proving that one's self is not wrong, evading accountability and responsibility, avoiding honest communication and accumulating data for proof of blame or innocence. The tendency to blame destroys trust and creates stress. Blaming creates an environment of fear. The world renowned quality expert, W. Edwards Deming, taught that we need to drive out all fear in order for organizations to work effectively. In order to drive out fear we need to drive in positive assumptions.

Most problems in organizations are systemic. That is, causes are built into the system we have created. Deming claimed that 94% of all problems were systemic and he attributed them to common causes. (*Out of The Crisis*, by W. Edwards Deming, M.I.T., 1982. Page 315) If most problems are systemic in their origin, then why do we spend so much time blaming individuals and groups?

First, most of us do not realize how much blaming is going on or that we are doing it. It becomes a way of life. The second problem is that we think that whoever is standing closest to a problem must be to blame for it. We are taken in by the illusion that there are simple, linear cause and effect relationships.

An example of this kind of thinking comes from a client of mine from several years ago. A manufacturing supervisor was upset with his people because the customer had sent back parts that did not meet the customer's specifications. He blamed his workers. He was sure the problem was their carelessness and poor work habits. His solution was to complain to them and criticize their work. This is a common occurrence in many organizations. I asked him a few questions:

- Were all of his people aware of the customer's specifications?
- Did they know how to set up their process in order to meet those specs?
- What were their inspection procedures?
- Were they applied appropriately to this shipment?
- Were all workers clear about their specific jobs and work expectations?
- Did all workers have the skills needed to produce the level of quality required?
- Was the equipment capable of producing the quality needed?
- Was there consistency in how each job was performed?

Most of these questions could not be answered well. There was little clarity and consistency in this system, so results tended to be inconsistent. Another question I asked was: "What impact do you think blaming and complaining have on their attitude and work product?" We cannot blame the people who work for us for poor quality when we have not taken the time to create a structure for success. The supervisor was accountable for the returned parts and so was his manager. The supervisor realized that he had the ability to empower the workers to do excellent work. It became his job to respond, and to make appropriate changes, with worker input, that would ensure that future shipments would be correct.

The illusion we create is that somehow blaming and complaining will make things better. Once we have blamed someone we feel compelled to "prove" it. We spend time and efforts building a case, amassing data, and defending our position. On the flip side, if we are blamed we spend time defending and justifying our decisions and actions. Imagine an organization full of people blaming, complaining, justifying, defending, and building cases against others. When would the real work get done?

If blaming is so futile, how can we avoid the blame game? There is only one place to start if your organization has blame as a way of life. Start with you. You begin to change the blaming culture by changing who you are being. Leaders must make a commitment not to blame or complain. If you must vent, do your venting to a trusted friend who is not your employee. Get it off your chest, recover your sanity, and remember that the problem is most likely in the system. The problem is an opportunity to make the system better. See problems as possibilities to be explored, not as opportunities to blame people.

We need to pay attention to how we talk to people. We need to be aware if we are critical, derogatory, sarcastic, or blaming. These conversations set a tone. These blaming and complaining conversations take us into a dead end. Instead of complaining about what is wrong, we can talk about the possibilities to be created.

Being a possibility thinker means much more than simply looking on the bright side of things. It means being committed to seeking and finding opportunities for greatness in every situation. It means looking for greatness in every person. This requires a positive assumption on our part — the assumption that there is greatness in every person. To shift into being a possibility thinker we need to assess where we are now. How does your way of being affect others?

- Have I taken the time to create positive relationships?

- Do I let people know that I value them?

- Am I aware of the needs, concerns, and issues of others?
- Am I responsive to their needs?
- Have I worked to create a structure that helps others succeed?
- Have I helped people get clarity on their mission, role, and the expected standards?
- Am I being true to myself?
- Do I give people honest feedback on their performance?
- Do I act quickly to correct problems?
- Do I listen to the people around me? Am I fully present when they talk to me?
- If I am not doing these things, what stops me? What is the payoff for me?
- Am I willing to give up the payoff for a chance to be more powerful — a chance to make my organization a better place?

These questions need to be asked in a spirit of exploration, not in a spirit of blaming. Each thing you are not doing is a possibility. If you are not taking the time to build positive relationships know this: Your current level of success will be greatly increased if you build strong, caring relationships with others. If people do not have much clarity, then a tremendous potential is available to you. With clarity of purpose, people will find more meaning in their work. Clarity and meaning motivate people to perform at higher levels.

The things we complain about are possibilities we can explore. For this reason we want to know what is wrong and what is not working. We must be careful not to blame the blamers in organizations. If it becomes politically incorrect to blame or complain, then people won't bring to the surface the problems they find. We need to encourage people to talk about what is wrong so we can act on it.

Each dissatisfaction is an opportunity to explore the assumptions underlying it. Complaints are usually symptoms of deeper issues. For example, a manager in an organization talked about having to "squeeze" information from another manager in another department. He presented this information as fact. Some people in the meeting viewed this comment as being negative and blaming. It was a blaming comment, but it was also an opportunity to create new possibilities.

Since the manager of the other department was present, we asked if information really did need to be "squeezed" from her. The resulting discussion revealed the following :

1. The manager who asked for the information did not say when he needed it.

2. He didn't say what the priority level was on the needed information.

3. The second manager didn't ask for a time frame or priority level. She simply put it on her "to do" list and eventually produced the information.

Both managers made assumptions about each other. How many other people sitting at the meeting had done the same thing? The discussion resulted in an agreement made between all of the managers to specify on all requests the following:

- What is needed?

- Who needs it?

- When is it needed by?

- Why is it needed?

- How or in what form is it needed?

- Where is it needed?

Lastly, we agreed that a response needed to be elicited on these requests. Communication is a two way responsibility, and all parties share in it. The managers in this organization have since adopted this practice with positive results.

Endless blaming and complaining in an organization can create feelings of hopelessness. The alternative is to handle complaints systematically in a way that does not threaten either the complainer or the one complained about.

Here are some steps that can be used to deal with complaints:

- Encourage complaints. Bring them to the surface and look at them.

- Look at what assumptions are beneath the complaints. In other words, what is the context for the person who is complaining?

- Question and test everyone's assumptions.

- Clarify what is wanted instead.

- Focus your energy on what you want.

Had the manager not brought up his issue, the group would not have improved their communication process. What began as a blaming remark turned into an opportunity to improve communications and relieve much frustration for the people in the organization. In the meeting energy shifted from blaming and complaining to coming up with communication guidelines that everyone could use. This group's vision was to increase responsiveness to each other in order to serve their customers better. Leaders can facilitate the shift from blaming to exploring possibilities by adopting a non-threatening stance regarding complaints. The intention is always to look for the possibilities within dissatisfaction and explore them fully. Dissatisfaction is a launching pad from which we can soar to success. For many leaders, this is a new way of being.

As a leader, your example teaches others how to act. The leader who is accountable and takes responsibility teaches her people to do the same. The leader who blames undermines her own authority and teaches people that they are not responsible. When we refuse to blame and choose to be accountable and responsible, we begin to discover our power. Focusing on what we can control— our thoughts, behaviors, and actions — makes us powerful. Small changes in how we relate to others, what we choose to believe about others, and opening ourselves to actually hearing what others have to say can create powerful results.

A leader's ability to make small changes within will influence those around him. His new way of being becomes a new way of doing. Others see the results and begin to make their own changes. Listening to complaints instead of defending or brushing them off is a small change that would have a strong effect. First, it tells the person who is complaining that they are important. Second, it becomes an opportunity to put your heads together to address the problem.

Usually when people complain we have one of three typical responses. We either join in and fall into the downward spiral together, politely listen, or ignore it because we are tired of hearing about it. Another option is to enter the reality of the person complaining.

Here is an example. Janet is complaining and Cheryl is listening. Their manager has just informed them of some last minute changes.

Janet complains, "Why do they always wait until the last minute?"

"It is last minute, but I think we can get it done," says Cheryl.

"That's not the point," counters Janet. "They should have given us these changes sooner."

"It would be easier. I know this last minute stuff really frustrates you."

"It frustrates me and it ticks me off. I'm tired of it. I wish we had some managers who actually knew what they were doing."

"Let's not jump to conclusions. It's true that we get a lot of last minute changes, but we don't know why. It could be the customer who is changing his mind. It could be a lot of things we don't know. Maybe we should try to find out."

"Why bother? Nothing will ever get done about it. Changes don't happen too fast around here."

"So, you'd like to see some changes, but you don't believe it can happen. Would you be willing to make a change?"

"There's nothing I can do about it."

"Well, that's the first change you can make. You can stop assuming that nobody cares and look at what we might do to improve this situation. You don't like last minute changes, and you feel frustrated and angry. What do you want?"

"I want timely information and respect, but you can't fight the system."

"We are the system, and we don't have to fight it. Look, maybe we can improve this situation and maybe we can't. If we can't we'll at least know that it's not anyone's fault. It's just a reality we need to accept. If we can change it, then we'll really feel good that we accomplished something."

"Are you always this positive?"

"Most of the time. Let's talk strategy."

Every leader is a teacher. Every person is a leader. Anyone can make the decision to be accountable and responsible, to treat others with care and respect, and to think in terms of possibilities. Moving beyond blaming and complaining opens up a world of possibilities.

Waiting for others to change, including those in higher positions, is an excuse. True leaders are people who initiate new ways of being. Culture change begins with one leader who has the will to create a vision and is willing to open to its possibilities.

Blaming is often a symptom of a lack of clarity. As an organization we need to know who we are. This begins with the mission. The mission is our reason for being. A good mission statement includes the following:

- What do we offer to those we serve?
- Who do we serve?
- How do we go about it?
- Why is it important?

A mission is ongoing. We find mission statements written in organization literature, framed in glass on office walls, and engraved on plaques. The mission needs to be engraved on the minds of everyone who is part of the organization. Everyone should have a clear idea of how their work contributes to the overall mission. Everyone should know who their customers are and be responsive to them.

Next to the mission is the vision. A vision describes the possibility we are becoming. It is a preferred future. If we were manifesting our vision right now, what would it look like, sound like, and feel like? People need to be made a part of the vision. This is done by giving them opportunities to offer feedback. We ask people constantly for their ideas. We use those ideas whenever possible. If we don't use a particular idea, we give feedback on why. Vision gives meaning to work and to being a part of a certain group.

If your organization does not have a vision, why not ask for one? Make a business case for having a clear direction. At the very least, you can create your own vision. Determine what you want to experience and how you want to feel. If you manage others, include them in your vision by talking about it with them. If you do not manage people, you can still have a vision. Share it with the people around you and the people you serve. A personal vision at work clarifies your direction each day. As you communicate and live your vision, people will come to know what you stand for and who you are.

In addition to mission and vision, some kind of guidance is needed. This guidance may come in the form of values, behavioral criteria, ground rules, norms, or guiding principles. Personally, I like guiding principles.

Guiding principles are ways of being that we consistently follow. Some guiding principles might be:

- People are first. We put the needs of people before all else.

- Timely responsiveness. We always respond to anyone who makes a request of us within 24 hours.

- Timeliness. We begin and end meetings on time. If it is impossible to arrive on time, we call in advance to inform the appropriate person.

- We expect the best. We do not settle for poor performance. We address people who are having performance problems compassionately, quickly and effectively.

People are motivated by meaning. When work has meaning, when we feel that what we are doing counts for something, when we are treated as valuable members of a group, then we become more powerful as an organization. The potential of the organization and its people is unleashed. Passion in the form of positive energy is allowed to flow. This creates an environment where people want to be present. If people are doing meaningful work, appreciated for that work, treated with high respect, and supported by a system that envisions excellence, there will be little ongoing blaming and complaining. Issues will be brought up and mined for their possibilities.

As a leader in an organization you need to know that you have the power to do this. You have the power to create and lead in a high-performing organization. It begins with your vision. Can you envision greatness in your organization? Your department? Your work area? Can you imagine that all of the people around you are world-class performers and team players? You must be able to imagine it to create it.

There is greatness within you and within others. We are each a possibility waiting to happen. Blaming is a denial of your greatness. It is the way that you pretend you are not powerful. Stop pretending and start envisioning. Once you envision, start being it. Your ability to be your vision makes you an inspiration to everyone else. There may be others who are not interested in greatness. Make it clear that the vision is where you are going. They may come along or not. Don't waste one minute complaining about people who aren't buying in. It is natural that people will resist.

Once your vision is clear and your way of being is in alignment, it is time to look at the system. Are there policies, processes, and ways of doing things that contradict the vision? Remove them and replace them with effective ways of doing things if you can. Ask people what is getting in their way and respond. Ask people what can be done to create greater alignment with the vision. If you do not have that authority, make an effective presentation to others who do have the authority. An effective presentation would be based on a clear understanding of their needs and wants.

A vision without people is incomplete. Teach people how to treat each other. Be a model of responsiveness to everyone. Apologize when you fall short. Teach people that settling for blaming is not only unacceptable, it is ineffective.

When things go wrong we often blame leaders. What we often fail to grasp is that our blaming is also part of the problem. We buy into the myth that top leaders can do whatever they want, that most important changes must come from the top down. The truth is that leaders are often frustrated when they cannot accomplish their goals. Leaders come up with new ideas and plans. They enthusiastically kick off new programs to improve morale, build team work, and empower employees. Employees make remarks like:

"He must have been to another one of those seminars."

"He must have read another book."

"Here we go with another flavor of the month."

Employees often blame leaders that nothing changes, yet refuse to make their own changes. Leaders implement programs and blame employees for not embracing them. The reason so many programs fail is that our thinking doesn't change. The content may be shifted through reengineering, team building, new rules, or management training, but the context is the same. Real change comes from changing our context. We change our context by being willing to look at it.

What assumptions do I make?
How do I know they are true?
Are these assumptions congruent with my vision?

Negative assumptions found in typical organizations include:

- Every day is the same.
- Management doesn't care about us.
- Employees only care about a paycheck.
- It will never work here.
- We already tried that and it didn't work.
- It's not my job.
- Those people don't know what they are doing.
- They don't listen.

These assumptions create a feeling of being powerless. They lead us to places of no solutions and no possibilities. Assumptions can be challenged. In fact, they should be challenged. It is important to hold some assumptions, but we shouldn't let assumptions hold us. Each of these statements assumes you are a victim. They assume blame. They prevent progress. Each of these assumptions can be turned into a statement of responsibility.

Assumption: Every day is the same.
Challenge: What needs to be different? What do we want?

Assumption: Management doesn't care about us.
Challenge: Do we care about them? Can we find ways to work together better and appreciate each other? What would be the benefits of this?

Assumption: Employees only care about a paycheck.
Challenge: How can we make work more meaningful for employees?

Anyone in an organization can affect the organizational context. Anyone can choose to stand up and lead. The trick is this: If your mindset, or context, is the same as the rest of the organization, and you stand up and try to convince others to change, you will probably fail. If your mindset or context is truly different, you have a vision, you are confident in yourself, and you are responsive to others, you can succeed. One person can influence a whole company, a country, or the world. A leader creates new, positive assumptions and teaches them to everyone else.

Summary: Each one of us is a leader. Each one of us has the power to lead from where we stand. We change organizations by changing the thoughts upon which they operate. Dissatisfaction is a launch pad from which we can soar to success. Our ability to question assumptions and create new possibilities makes us effective leaders.

16 Taking The "Dys" Out Of Dysfunctional

To say something is dysfunctional is to say it isn't working. To call a person dysfunctional is to say they are unable to communicate openly and honestly with others. A relationship is dysfunctional if the participants are unable to communicate effectively. Usually boundaries are not clear. People attempt to get their needs met through manipulation. People intimidate, verbally attack, avoid conflict, play the "poor me" game, ignore each other, excessively complain, and act in passive-aggressive ways. Passive-aggressive behaviors are ones I may use to "get you" without being direct. I may withhold information, plant seeds of discontent with others, delay in responding to your requests, and generally do things to make you pay.

We have all been dysfunctional at one time or another. Labeling people and organizations as dysfunctional is not productive. The question is: "Am I being functional in this moment? Am I communicating openly and honestly. Am I responding to you as a person as well as respecting myself as a person?" The cause of dysfunctionality is fear. We fear job loss, rejection, embarrassment, being yelled at, conflict, hurting others' feelings, exposing our emotions, being seen as incompetent, getting too close to others, and a host of other such fears.

The outcome of dysfunctionality is denial. There are problems, but we don't want to talk about them. Or, we talk about the problems, but we don't want to talk about the real causes. Instead, we go into survival mode. We develop strategies that will help us keep our jobs, move up in the organization, survive each day, avoid blame, or keep us in the good graces of those we think we need to please. We call this "normal", and we accept it as reality. Viktor Frankl wrote in his book, *Man's Search for Meaning*: "Abnormal behavior in an abnormal situation is normal." Normal in this case, is not healthy, or even desirable. In many families and organizations, it's all we know.

If you have read this far in this book, you already have a good idea of how to be more functional. You know to stop blaming and being a victim. You know to be responsive to other people. You know how to acknowledge emotions — yours and those of others. You know the importance of not being in denial about what is happening, and to address it with compassion and directness. But, what if you are the only person like this? What if everyone else is "dysfunctional"? Everyone else is scared, or blaming.

It is easy to get drawn into the dysfunction when you are surrounded by it. It is difficult to be blameless when everyone else is blameful. You aren't getting any support. You, who understand these ideas, are a light, a beacon of hope for the others who surround you. It seems like they are constantly trying to dim your light, to cover it up. You end up frustrated, disappointed, and feeling like a victim. You are not a victim. The principles of clarity and responsiveness still apply here. What do you want?

Your frustration is a sign you are focusing on what you don't want. You have to be clear about the possibilities you want to create, and refuse to accept anything less. You focus on what you want by reminding yourself about it every day. You look for small improvements and celebrate them. You address negativity with clarity, responsiveness, and firmness. To accomplish this you must learn to handle your fear. Three things, all of which we have already discussed, will help you.

1. Listen to your intuitive voice. Listening to and following your intuitive voice works. It tells you to respond to people and to situations. When you follow it you feel good. When you ignore it you feel bad. Practice pausing and listening before you act or speak about something important. Fear is caused by the illusion that your well-being is given by other people or things. There is a treasure of

wisdom within you. If you are not accustomed to following your intuition, practice by using it with small things. Build your confidence in this way. Listening within will help you to clarify who you are.

2. We have discussed the importance of responsiveness. You need to shift your attention to the needs and concerns of others. This is not about making others happy or pleasing them. It is about listening within and responding in a way that meets their needs in this moment. It means not avoiding conflict, but addressing how someone feels. When someone is angry we need not cower in fear, nor do we need to shout them down. Our focus becomes one of deep concern for the person. This is compassion.

3. You may find yourself in fear and discomfort. Decide what you want instead. Create it in your mind. How would you feel? Each morning before coming to work, envision what you want. Feel the feelings you want to have. Envision straightforward, compassionate conversations.

"In order to overcome your own fears you have to start first by showing compassion to others. Once you have started treating people with compassion, kindness and understanding, then your fears dissipate. It's that straightforward," said Nobel Peace Prize winner Aung Sang Suu Kyi in her book, *The Voice of Hope*.

When you find yourself in the midst of insanity remind yourself that you don't have to join in. Breathe. Take a break if you need it. Get clear about what would be the most healthy response on your part, and then respond. Accept that people are where they are, and you cannot make them be different. Know that they are acting out of their best thinking in this moment.

Sometimes you just need the right words. The following sample situation will be of help.

Joan works in an office with seven other women. Their boss is a man who uses intimidation to rule over his domain. He raises his voice; speaks crossly to people; criticizes people in front of their coworkers; and is critical when others challenge him. Joan is not afraid of him, but everyone else is. In staff meetings, Joan will bring up issues and speak her mind. The boss usually reacts with anger. The other women tell Joan to stop bringing up problems. They don't like the yelling.

At the Monday morning meeting, Joan did it again. She brought up a sensitive issue, and the boss exploded. The other women all looked down at the table in fear. The outburst went on for a few minutes, then he changed the subject. Nothing was resolved. Joan decided she had had enough. She scheduled a meeting with the boss.

Joan began, "Thanks for taking the time to meet with me."

Her boss responded, "That's okay. What's this about?"

"I like my job, and I think I do it well. At the same time there are a few issues around here that make both my job and yours more difficult. If we could solve these issues we'd be a lot better at what we do, and both you and I would be more successful."

"I'm listening."

"First, this morning's meeting. You are my manager. I want to work with you to make us successful. I am willing to do whatever it takes to make us better. What I am not willing to do is be yelled at by you. I am a professional and an adult, as are you. I will not be treated like a subhuman. Your yelling doesn't motivate me to improve. I wanted to tell you this privately, and if it happens again, I'm going to call you on it right in front of everybody."

"Is that it?"

"No, I'm just getting started. You scare the other women in the office. They are afraid to bring anything to you for fear that you will yell at them. That means we avoid problems. We don't address issues so they get worse. Like the issue I brought up this morning. You yelled at me for bringing it up, yet nothing was done about it. It's still a problem. It's still affecting our business. Having problems doesn't make you a bad manager, but I'm afraid that avoiding them may make both you and all of us look bad. I can't believe that's what you would want."

"We have too many mistakes around here and they shouldn't be happening. This isn't what I want and you know it!"

"Whoa! Hold up. You're doing it again."

"Doing what?"

"Raising your voice. Yelling. Hey, I'm not the enemy here."

"Well, it makes me angry."

"What makes you most angry about it?"

"I have to keep repeating myself."

"I know you're angry. I get angry, too. And, you're right, there are too many mistakes. Tell me what you would like to see happening instead. Be specific."

There is no guarantee as to how the boss will respond. He may see the light immediately and start to work cooperatively with Joan. His respect for her will grow, because she has made her boundaries clear. He may respect her and continue to give disrespect to the others. He may get angry and yell at her again. He may avoid her from this point on. When you decide to be clear, honest, and responsive to someone, you invite them to do the same. You increase the chances that they will respond positively. It is also possible that they will refuse the invitation. Either way, you will feel better that you took responsibility and interacted with compassion.

Joan's focus was not on changing her boss. It was on changing her way of being. Blaming and being a victim were no longer acceptable. Her willingness to communicate honestly, compassionately, and clearly creates the potential for a healthier work environment.

As an executive coach I have seen people do a complete turnaround after one or two conversations with me. I have also seen some people completely reject what I offered. Fortunately, the latter is much more rare. What it comes down to is that you have to be willing to walk away. If your security and well-being is tied to a job or a relationship, then you subject yourself to the whims of other people. This makes you powerless. People often blame and complain about their relationships with bosses, colleagues, spouses, and friends, but don't do anything about it.

If you have chosen to give up being yourself in order to keep a job, keep a spouse, or keep a friend, you cannot blame them. You make the decision to allow people to treat you the way they do. As Dr. Phillip McGraw states in his well known book, *Life Strategies*: "You teach people how to treat you."

When people blame and complain they create the illusion that everyone else is insane and that they are okay. If you are in a family or an organization where abnormal has become normal, where communications are strained, where conflicts are not dealt with, where people are denying problems, then you are part of it. If you wake up one day and realize that this situation (family, relationship, workplace) is insane, then you need to make a move. Own it. Own your part in perpetuating the insanity. Decide what you want to have instead.

When you stop blaming and complaining and start taking responsibility your conversations change. You no longer participate or stand quietly by while people blame others. You ask responsible questions: "Have you talked to him about that issue? Have you tried approaching it differently? Have you asked him how he sees this situation? What would you like to see happen instead?" You stop reinforcing the blaming through your participation or your silence, and you challenge it. This may not make you popular at first.

At this point you may actually be the only sane person in an insane group. You are now abnormal, and abnormal, in this case, is healthy. Your job isn't to fix everyone else, because you can't. Your job is to be yourself, to speak honestly, to be helpful, and to keep being responsive. If you stay the course one of two things will happen.

1. Things may get worse and people will reject you. If this happens, don't resist it. Allow people to be who they are. You need to start looking for a new situation that is as healthy as you are. If you don't want to leave, you need to carve out a place for yourself where you feel good. Don't blame people for who they are being. Focus on creating an experience that feels good for you. Offer sincere positive comments frequently and maintain healthy boundaries.

2. Things will get better. Your ability to be clear, compassionate and honest will inspire others to do the same. The group will begin to change for the better. The organization will attract healthier people. Unhealthy people will leave.

Certainly it takes courage to be honest. It takes courage to look at yourself and acknowledge the part you have played in creating the current state. You may be thinking that you can't do these things because you need this job, this relationship, this friend. This is a limiting thought. Challenge it. What are alternatives you can pursue? Why do you think this job is the only one you can do? Why do you think this relationship is the only one for you?

This is not to say that leaving is the answer. There are two kinds of leaving. In the first type, you are clear about what you want. You see that you cannot create it in this present situation. You do not judge the people around you for this. You let go of anger and resentment, wish them well, and move on.

The second way is to go away angry. You blame and resent people for not changing. If you don't work out your anger and resentment, you are likely to recreate a similar situation. This is why some people marry the same personality (different person) two, three and four times. People leave workplaces upset with THEM only to find another THEM waiting at the next job.

Remember, in all of your relationships, conflicts, situations, struggles, and experiences there has been one common denominator—you. Look at your past experiences and notice the patterns. Notice what your tendencies have been. What has been your context in each of these situations? Challenge it. "In what ways did I choose to be the victim? How did I affect others with my way of being? How often did I betray myself? Did I see others truly, or as objects? Did I spend my time blaming and complaining, or taking positive action? Did I have a clear vision about what I wanted? Did I communicate clearly to others about what I expected?" Asking these questions about yourself makes you functional and healthy. Do not allow yourself to fall into the downward spiral of self-blaming. It is a waste of time to label yourself or another as dysfunctional. Start functioning right now.

The key thing to remember, if you are in a dysfunctional situation, is that you are not changing other people. You cannot change them, so don't blame yourself if they don't change. Clarify who you are. Focus on what you want to create. Respond to others. Refuse to be a victim of the dysfunctionality. Look for what is highest and best in people, and serve that. Serving others does not mean being a people pleaser. People pleasing is something you do for yourself. You keep others happy so that you feel okay. Serving others is about meeting their needs.

As a pleaser, I will treat my boss with kindness so that he won't get mad or he will like me. As a server, I treat my boss with respect. If he doesn't like me, I ask him what the problem is. I listen to him and offer an honest response. My intent as a pleaser is for others to like me or approve of me. As a server of people I forego needing to be liked, and focus on being real, effective, and fully present with people. If I feel I must stay in a group of people who don't function well, then I must find outside groups that are healthy in order to support my own health.

It is futile to blame people in dysfunctional groups. They usually don't know what they are doing. All they know is that they feel compelled to think and act in certain ways. Your resistance to them only serves to support their dysfunction. If you want out of the game, you have to stop playing. Stop blaming. Stop criticizing. Stop thinking that they must change. Stop plotting and planning. Accept people where they are right now. Speak your truth with compassion. Live from your values. Your intent to be healthy will affect others.

I was called into an organization to coach the manager of a very dysfunctional unit of a relatively healthy organization. I found the people to be in chaos. The manager criticized people in public and found ways to make life difficult for anyone who disagreed with her. I interviewed people and found them to be stressed and unhappy. Many were afraid of what she might do to them (yell at them, fire them, embarrass them). Many of them felt hope because this change process had begun.

Survey results from the employees provided data for changes that needed to be made. I began my coaching process in good faith, focusing on the "health" that I saw within the manager. After two or three weeks she suddenly rebelled against the process, obtained an attorney, and demanded that both her manager and I leave her alone. There was plenty of documentation showing that a change was needed in this department. She ended up losing her job. A new manager was hired. The new manager was emotionally healthy and capable of facilitating the healing that was needed in this department.

At face value, my coaching was a failure. Yet, the end result of the process was a success. I knew going in that the manager might resist. What was learned from this situation? First, you cannot fix people. You offer help and they choose. People have free will. They have the choice to remain in their dysfunction, or to work toward reclaiming their health. Second, you do not protect people from the consequences they create. It was sad that she lost her job. Sometimes people need to hit bottom before they can start to look at themselves. Third, you keep the vision in mind, regardless of the dysfunction that may be going on around you. Our vision for that department was that of a harmonious place where people could enjoy their work and offer excellence. This we accomplished.

The fourth lesson is about fear. You cannot allow fear to drive your thinking or decisions. Whenever fear is driving you, you become part of the dysfunction. It is important to recognize when you are fearful so that you can shift your thinking. Thoughts create fear. Whenever you find yourself in a dysfunctional situation you are faced with your own emotional reactions to the emotions of others. Do other people's expressions of anger make you uncomfortable? This is your work. When others become stressed, or angry, or uncomfortable, it doesn't mean that you have to fix them. Tell yourself that it is okay that someone else feels angry or upset. Ask yourself how best you can respond.

If you find that most of the groups that you belong to are dysfunctional, ask yourself why that is. What is it about these groups that attracts you? If you are not happy with groups like this, what would you like instead? Envision your preference, and decide how you want to feel in a group. Imagine it and write it down. Envision it and start looking for signs of health, both in groups you are already in, and in new groups you may join. Focus your thinking on what you want. If you are pouring your energy into struggling with the dysfunction around you, you are only perpetuating the struggle. Healthy relationships where people actually talk to each other, listen to each other, and respond effectively do exist. If you have the intent, you can create healthy relationships both at work and in your personal life. Your increased mental health will attract to you others who are equally healthy.

Summary: Fear prevents us from functioning. Get control of your fears by refusing to allow them to run your life. Compassion and understanding will help you to become less fearful. Your intent to create healthy relationships will succeed as you become what you intend.

17 Self-Blaming

Blaming yourself usually leads to guilt or shame. Guilt comes from punishing yourself for something you did or did not do. Shame comes from punishing yourself for the person you think you are. Both guilt and shame are highly overrated as motivators for positive behavior. On the flip side, when we are in the emotional state of anger, we want the other person to feel guilty or ashamed. We want to see the guilt, to hear them say how sorry they are, and to know that they have suffered for what they have done to us. You have only to pick up the daily newspaper to read about someone somewhere who wants to see someone else punished for what they have done.

We think it will make us feel better if someone suffers for what they have done to us. Initially it may seem to make us feel better. "At least justice was served!" we say when someone is punished for what they did. Does it help us to heal? Does it help us to recover from whatever happened? Perhaps, it helps indirectly. Now that the perpetrator is punished we can stop obsessing about them being punished. Guilt makes promises it can never deliver. If we succeed in making another feel guilty, it is never enough. We want them to feel guilty again and again. Our need for their guilt is insatiable. It interferes with our healing. Only letting go of the blame will help us to heal.

I recall being quite successful, in my younger years, at encouraging another person to feel guilty. I had only to flash my "hurt look" to initiate the guilt response. Others often became angry when they felt the guilt, and did or said more hurtful things. In those cases, my desire for their guilt backfired. "Success" in my guilt-making would have had the other person acting apologetic and going out of their way to make me feel better. This was not as satisfying as I thought it would be. It was often uncomfortable. I discovered that all I really wanted was for the other person to care— to see me as a person.

Apologizing for hurtful behavior is certainly a good thing. Playing a penitent role afterwards is not. Guilt and shame diminish us. If I feel guilty for something I have done to you, my guilt diminishes me and poisons our relationship. My guilt causes me not to be myself around you. It causes me to get angry at you because my guilt is never enough. You always seem to want more. Guilt has me telling myself I am not good enough to be your parent, your spouse, your manager, or your employee. "Not good enough" by virtue of my guilt is my way of being when I am with you. I want to feel good, but I deny myself feeling good. As a guilty person I do not deserve to feel good. My goal becomes not feeling good with you. My other goal becomes proving that I deserve your forgiveness.

This is one of the biggest problems with guilt. As a guilty person, you are constantly trying to earn others' forgiveness. You want others to see that you really are good, that you really are worthy. At the same time, you are acting as if you are unworthy, and that you do not deserve others' forgiveness.

I played this game years ago when I did some things that hurt my children's feelings. I was embarrassed at my behavior. I was disappointed in the kind of father I had been. I felt guilty and unworthy to be their father. Conventional wisdom might say this is a good thing. It wasn't. My inability to forgive myself made it difficult for me to truly see my children. I was so caught up in my pain that it was difficult for me to see their pain.

As a parent, I looked for ways to impress my children with my qualifications as a parent. When it came to actual parenting, I held back, afraid of their disapproval, afraid that once again, I would prove my unworthiness. My guilt often kept me from being a truly good parent. I was hesitant, because I didn't want to intensify the feeling of guilt. I avoided my guilt by avoiding being a parent.

When we are blaming ourselves we diminish ourselves whenever we are around those who are the objects of our guilt. How can they help but see a small person when they look at us? Self-blaming takes us into a downward spiral. No matter what we do, the guilt is always there. We mistakenly believe that our release comes from them forgiving us. How do we move beyond self-blaming ?

If my self-blaming is about something I did to another, I must realize that my context has not changed. When I did things that hurt my children, I failed to fully consider their needs. I was wrapped up in myself. In my guilt, I am still failing to fully consider their needs. In the guilt state, I am still wrapped up in myself. Guilt is not about what we have done to others. It is only about what we are doing to ourselves. In guilt I need you to punish me or to release me. The problem with guilt is that my focus is still on me. Guilt, or self-blaming, is a sign that I have not learned anything from what I did.

I cannot be free to be a great parent until I stop blaming myself. I cannot stop blaming until I learn to stop thinking about myself so much. The motivation for ending the self-blaming is twofold: One, I get to feel better. Two, in fully considering the needs of my children, I help them to feel better. Now, when I am with them, I am less concerned with my image as a father. I am more concerned about them and the relationship. For me, this process of moving beyond self-blaming to a better relationship happened in stages. My willingness to hear their needs and concerns and their willingness to speak with complete honesty helped us both to heal.

When we are stuck in the guilt, we don't want to hear how the other person is feeling. It is too painful. We avoid our guilt, and we allow it to fester. We do not move beyond self-blaming by avoiding it. The guilt we have must be faced and felt. The pain of guilt may be intense. We may think that it is too much. After all, that is why we have been avoiding it. The pain is actually cleansing. When we allow deep, painful emotions to surface, we create the potential for self-healing.

The greatest gift I can give to my children is not to feel guilty for my failures as a parent. The greatest gift is to listen to them, and to be a whole and worthy person —to be an example that they can look up to. Every child wants to be able to think well of their parents. When parents stop avoiding their guilt, face it, and actually listen to their children, relationships heal. I have known too many parents of teenage to adult children who feel guilty and defensive toward their children, and as a consequence, rarely speak to them. These parents tell themselves that the children are being unreasonable and unforgiving. This may be true, but it is not the children who are the problem. Their way of being reflects back to the parent the guilt that is already there.

Learning comes from changing context. Guilt comes from a limited context that doesn't allow us to see the reality of the other person. Guilt is like having our heads in the sand. Relationships are in peril. Opportunities for healing them abound. We can't see either, because avoiding the pain has been our goal. We overwork, drug ourselves, watch too much television, or utilize any number of escapes from the pain of our guilt. When I take the risk and say: "It's okay to experience the pain. I can face this. I can listen to the feelings of those who feel hurt by me. I can seek to understand their reality and feel compassion for them," I can heal.

Compassion is the willingness to see people as they are. True compassion does not include pity or feeling sorry for someone. Compassion means that we accept others' reality and refuse to judge them for it. We appreciate others' experience as a human being. Compassion is our capacity to respond to others and to help them get what they need. Compassion has us listening to others fully. It does not mean being nice, being lenient, or excusing bad behavior. Compassion is responsiveness.

In dealing with guilt, compassion is given to ourselves. We can only exercise this compassion if we are willing to experience the pain of our guilt. When we feel guilt, our hope is that we can redeem ourselves. Redemption does not come from guilt. Redemption comes from compassion. Coming from guilt, all attempts to redeem myself have me using others to try to lose the guilt. Coming from compassion, I redeem myself by acting in ways that are truly helpful for others. Redemption comes from focusing on the needs of others.

I redeem myself as a parent whenever I fully listen to my children and accept their present moment reality. If my children refuse to talk to me (which is not true in my case), then I accept their feelings as valid for them. I can still be compassionate in my thinking toward them. I can still look for opportunities to respond to them as people. In being compassionate, in listening to them, and in caring more about their well-being than I care about my image as a parent, I am, in this moment, a good parent.

This is the key to transcending all self blaming. Forget about who you thought you were, and be who you want to be now. Admit mistakes, learn from them, and become the person you want to be. Be in this present moment where making changes is possible, rather than immersing yourself in the past that cannot be changed. I have spent a good deal of writing space discussing parenting issues because so many of us have them. The principles discussed here are universal. They apply to all situations of self-blaming.

Shelley gave a presentation in front of a group. From the group's perspective she did a passable job. Information was communicated and received. From Shelley's point of view, it was horrendous. It was her worst experience as a public speaker. She forgot several things she meant to say. She was often hesitant. She felt very nervous. She blamed herself and felt deep disappointment in her performance. She decided to take a break from speaking for a while.

Her sense of disappointment and shame is painful. The mere thought of speaking in front of people brings up these feelings. She can only avoid the pain by not speaking. Avoidance is resistance. As long as Shelley resists her speaking experience and the feelings surrounding it, the pain will persist. Instead, Shelley can respond to this experience. The pain of this "failure" is an incredible opportunity for Shelley to become an excellent speaker. The opportunity is taken by being willing to feel the pain and look at the experience.

A reality check could be helpful. Was the presentation as bad as she thought it was? She can ask people who were in her audience for feedback. What value did you get from the presentation? What was missing from it? What would have made it more relevant, interesting, or helpful? She can accept this feedback without being defensive and without offering explanations. She can use the information for improvement.

Shelley's disappointment has her right in the middle of what she doesn't want. She doesn't want to feel inadequate. She doesn't want to feel not confident. She doesn't want to feel disappointed. The question is: "How does she want to feel?" She wants to feel confident and competent. She wants to feel like she is on a roll or in the zone. She wants to feel at ease, powerful, and clear. This is what she wants. In order to get what she wants, she needs to focus her thought and emotion on it.

Wallowing in disappointment and feeling small has her focusing on what she doesn't want. Imagining herself as a confident speaker, and taking actions to create that ability in herself, have her focusing on what she does want. Moving beyond blaming, Shelley creates her vision, assesses where her abilities are right now, and creates a plan for realizing her vision. Whenever we experience a failure we always have a choice. We can become victims of our own blaming, or we can use the experience to become powerful and successful in what we do.

Shame is the most debilitating kind of self-blaming. Shame tells me that there is something wrong with who I am. I did what I did because there is something inherently wrong with me. Or, there is something inherently wrong with me, which is why people do bad things to me. In a state of shame, self-blaming is automatic. We accept mistreatment and mistreat ourselves because of shame. The way to move beyond shame begins with recognizing it isn't real. It is something we, or others, have made up. That being the case we can make a decision to love and accept ourselves exactly as we are. In making this decision, the self-blaming reactions are less automatic.

As we begin to feel ashamed, we can become aware of the emotion, and remind ourselves of the decision we have made. We need not do battle with this tendency to feel ashamed. We can recognize it and accept it. It is merely our past programming. We can remind ourselves that this is not how we want to be. We can refocus our attention on our vision and goals for ourselves.

We experience situations like Shelley's because of a sense of shame. We are afraid of being exposed in front of others. If we make a mistake, what will be exposed? We fear that the negative and critical thoughts we have about ourselves will be confirmed in the reactions of others. As a result, many people hold back their gifts and talents fearing embarrassment and rejection. If you love and accept yourself, the opinions of others are less important. The opinions of others can offer valuable feedback on our actions, but need not be accepted as comments about who we are.

What are you blaming yourself for? Are you willing to move beyond blaming? Are you willing to face the pain and create something better for yourself? You can. It isn't easy, but staying in guilt and shame isn't easy either. Painful emotions involving guilt and shame can set the tone for a lifetime. Imagine my relationship with my now grown-up children if I were still running away from guilt. Imagine Shelley spending the rest of her life being afraid of making public presentations. Imagine all of us, including you, being powerful enough to do what we want to do.

Self-blaming is the result of a focus on what we think is wrong with us. When we continually tell ourselves what is wrong we magnify it. One thing we can do is to start offering ourselves unconditional positive regard. This means that we refuse to place conditions on our self-regard. We deal with mistakes honestly. Mistakes are not reasons to blame self or others, but opportunities to reflect and to make necessary changes. We can look at so-called failures and mistakes as a possibility thinker. As long as you are breathing there are possibilities for you. If you are extremely self-critical, take yourself off the hook. Spend more time focusing on your successes. Deal with errors honestly without attaching negative meaning to them. In other words, learn from mistakes. Repair damage with people. Guilt trips make lousy vacations both for you and everyone around you.

Earlier, in Chapter Eight, we discussed self-deception and self-betrayal, two concepts introduced by the Arbinger Institute in *Leadership and Self-Deception*. Self-betrayal is when we fail to respond to another and then project the blame on to them. Most, if not all, blaming is projection. That is, we feel guilty but pin the blame on someone else. It is an attempt to make ourselves feel better. If I can blame you, I can maintain my image as a good person. If I can maintain my image of self I can avoid pain and maybe feel better about myself. It doesn't work, but we do it anyway hoping that it will. Therefore, another way to move beyond blaming is to learn how to love and accept ourselves. As we more completely love and accept ourselves, even though we have made mistakes, there is less of a need to blame. Instead of blaming self or others, we simply respond to people and situations effectively. For most of us, this is no easy task. Self-acceptance is a decision you make. It is a discipline you follow. It requires you to pay attention to what you are telling yourself.

If you listen to the news regularly you will notice the repetitious negative sound bites. We constantly hear about crime, terrorism, bad weather, people criticizing each other, and conflict. We hear the same negative messages over and over again. Much of the news is fear-based. In our minds we produce our own news show. We tell ourselves the same repetitious negative thoughts again and again. These, too, are usually fear-based. What are your internal sound bites? Here are a few self-blaming sound bites:

"I am not good enough."

"I never win anything."

"I hate these thighs (or stomach, or breasts, or whatever body parts you dislike)."

"It's not fair! Why am I always in this position?"

"I have to be good at this to be accepted."

"Why am I always struggling to make ends meet? What is wrong with me?"

"I can't believe how stupid I am!"

"What is the matter with me?"

You could probably add a few of your own to this list. We have to become aware of the voice in our mind always criticizing, blaming, whining, telling ourselves the many ways that we don't measure up. Challenge the voice. Declare your intent to completely love and accept yourself exactly as you are. Catch yourself saying that you must have money, or status, or certain relationships in order to be acceptable. Don't let your mind get away with these automatic defeating thoughts. You already are acceptable. To tell yourself this message takes faith—faith that even though you may not feel it at this moment, it is true. It also takes courage, because going against the grain of your previous thinking isn't easy. However, it is worth it.

When critical and self-blaming thoughts arise, you feel bad. Emotions are your body's response to your thinking. You are not your emotions. You experience emotions. Observe your thinking and make choices regarding what you think about. The final three chapters in this book will include ideas and methods for releasing negative emotions.

Often guilt and shame are deeply embedded in our way of being. In these cases therapy can be helpful. In addition to conventional therapists (psychologists, social workers, etc.) there are many alternative therapies available. Effective energy therapists, for example, may help people to release emotional blockages to personal well-being. Choose your professional healers based on your intuition and knowledge. Ultimately, your ability to move beyond self-blaming depends on your intention. Your persistent intention and willingness will lead you in the right direction.

The people in our lives serve as mirrors of who we think we are. Unresolved issues are sparked by the words and behaviors of others. This is often most evident in family relationships.

Summary: Self-blame will not redeem you. Compassion will redeem. Self-blame is a focus on the past. Focus on who you want to be now. Self-blame becomes blaming toward others, because we project our guilt. We must learn to quiet the critical voice in our minds and practice self-acceptance.

18 Blaming in Family Relationships

Moving beyond blaming with our families can be one of the most difficult challenges. Often our attitudes toward family members are deeply etched in our minds and in our physiology. Through constant practice our blaming thoughts become habitual. Our bodies react to these thoughts with the emotions of anger, shame, guilt, resentment, and a host of others. Negative reactions to family members are literally built into our physiology. When you think about certain family members your body knows what to do. Chemical messengers are sent throughout your body in response to certain thoughts. When your mother gets that certain tone in her voice, you automatically feel resentment and anger. When your spouse looks at you with that certain look, you automatically feel irritation.

Of course, positive emotions are built in also. Interactions that call forth positive memories from the past will elicit feelings of being loved, nurtured, and supported. The point is, whether we are appreciating or blaming a family member, we often don't have to think about it consciously. The mental and emotional reactions come automatically. This is the challenge. I may tell myself I am going to appreciate my spouse, my parent, or my child, but the moment they do something that is connected to an unpleasant memory, my body reacts with emotion. My negative thoughts kick in and I have forgotten my resolve. It is difficult to overcome the negative emotions built into our physiology, but there is hope.

Is there someone in your family you blame? A son you don't talk to? A daughter who is estranged? An ex-spouse who left you? A parent who hurt you? Many people carry blame toward some family member.

This kind of blaming is painful and turns us into victims. Are you the victim of a negative family relationship? If so, your anger and hurt may have been valid. You have the right to be angry or hurt. Maybe you needed to be angry or hurt to motivate you to get out of an unhealthy situation. How about right now? Is your blaming helping you to live a happy, successful life? Does it help you to be healthy and positive in your present relationships?

For most of us, carrying blame is a great burden. Like a condemned building, it casts an ugly shadow over everything in the neighborhood of our lives. Blaming creates more pain for us than for the person we blame. Thoughts and feelings of blame are barriers to success and experiencing joy. They imprison us within walls of illusions. The illusions are the stories we tell ourselves about these relationships.

Once I found myself telling an old story about my father. Years ago he had made some insensitive and discouraging remarks about my creative abilities. I listened to myself, and I heard the hurt in my voice. My story's theme was about a mean dad who didn't encourage his son. What were the implications of that story? Was it that I would be more successful today if he had encouraged me? Was it a comparison to show that I had become a much better father than he ever was?

Some questions came to mind. Why was I holding on to a story that was over thirty years old? Why was it that I could still feel the hurt feelings of that long-ago moment? Was that how I really wanted to define myself now? How was that story helping me to be happy and successful today? I thought I had resolved my father issues long ago. In this instance, a negative memory was sparked. As soon as I heard myself I didn't like the person I was being. I didn't want to be a victim of my father, nor did I want to blame myself for reliving that distant memory. I let it go.

My father and I had a blaming relationship. As a child I always felt criticized by him. As I grew older I became very critical of him. I blamed him for what I saw as his inability to relate and to communicate. As a result, it was not until I was almost thirty that I could feel comfortable around him. It was then that I made a decision to accept him as he was, and to stop looking for his approval. I learned to care about the father I had rather than continually looking for the father I wished I had.

At some point in time you have to grow up. You have to give up being the hurt child of your parents. They did what they did based on their view of the world at the time. That was who they were. Who are you? Are you the product of your parents and their treatment of you, or are you your own creation?

If you see yourself as the product of your past experience, think again. Aren't you the product of your accumulated wisdom? It's not what you have experienced that makes you who you are. It is what you have learned that makes you who you are.

I grew up in a home where my physical needs were always met. I always had enough food and clothing. I was encouraged to do well in school. I was taught to respect others and to work for what I wanted. My parents did many good things for me. The one thing my parents were unable to do was verbalize their love and appreciation. I never heard the words "I love you" in my childhood. As a young adult I blamed both of my parents for this. I thought that they should have been able to express love. After thirty years of building and practicing my blaming attitude toward my parents an opportunity came for me to move beyond blaming.

My mother needed an operation. I found myself feeling both concern and great love for her the night before her surgery. I called her on the phone to wish her well. I had the thought, call it my inner voice, to tell her that I loved her. I said those important words to my mother and she said them back to me. After the phone conversation I found myself in an emotional state. It was as if my body was releasing years of emotion through my tears. I had no control over this. Afterwards I felt light and content. In the moment that I said those words, I grew up. I was no longer the hurt child , but an independent adult.

There was another voice within me that I did not listen to. It was the voice in my mind that said, "Why should I say that to her? She has never said it to me." Had I followed that voice I would have justified my inaction with more blaming toward my mother. Fortunately I chose to listen to my Inner Voice instead.

As a result my mother and I have developed a good relationship. I feel comfortable being honest with her. Although I initiated that first expression of love, she has initiated those words many times since then. I cannot guarantee that everyone's parent will be as receptive as my mother was, but it doesn't matter. Eventually I told my father that I loved him, and he didn't respond. I am still happy that I told him. My goal was to let him know how I felt, not to change him. I accomplished my goal.

Who in your family do you have an icy relationship with? Who do you refuse to talk to? What is your story about that? Who are you being in this blaming state? Are you justifying your way of being by telling yourself how bad, unreasonable, rude, or disrespectful the other person is? How have you affected them over the years? Has anything you have done hurt them?

Letting go of blame frees you. It doesn't mean you have to hang out with them. Let's face it, sometimes certain family members are not the people you would choose as your friends. Letting go of blame means you release your need for them to change. You accept them as they are. You decide what you want and you make your decision clear. If your uncle tends to get drunk at family gatherings, you don't blame him for that. At the same time, you don't have to invite him to your house until he gives up drinking. It's your house. Your blaming will not help him get sober. Your clear boundaries and caring attitude may help him.

If your parent seriously abused you (physical, sexual, and/or extreme emotional), that's certainly justifiable blame, isn't it? Yes, it is justifiable, but does it help you? If he or she gets credit for ruining your life, how does that help you? As a child, your parent had total power over you. Your parent was 100% responsible for anything he did to you. But now, as an adult, you are 100% responsible for your well-being. Your healing demands that you stop blaming the parent who hurt you. Why did he do it? Sometimes there are no good reasons for the terrible things people do to each other. People who hurt other people do it out of their own pain. That's not an excuse. It's a reality. Stop looking to your parent for your value as a person. Your value is within you, and cannot be altered by the acts of a parent or anyone else.

If your parent did terrible things to you, you can stop blaming. This doesn't mean that you let him baby-sit your children. What level of involvement this person has in your life or your children's lives is based on issues of safety and well-being. Releasing blame means you no longer allow this person to have power over you. You do not allow them to make you feel guilty, hurt, or angry. If you do experience these feelings, you become aware of them, make decisions that help you and your children to maintain safety and well-being, and let the emotion go. The emotion is a signal that something isn't right at the time, i.e., they aren't behaving responsibly, you aren't listening to your intuition, or your family is at risk. Listen to the emotion, and take responsible action.

Most family rifts aren't about serious abuse issues. Some event happens where somebody says something, and that's it. Both parties feel they are the victim. Both parties are angry and hurt. Neither party is willing to see their own responsibility in the matter. "I realize I'm not perfect," she says, "but I don't hear her admitting to her part in this." We can challenge the position we have taken by asking ourselves:

- Was I untrue to myself in any way?
- Was I not completely honest in this situation?
- If so, am I willing to repair this?
- Did I listen fully with the intention of understanding him/her?
- Was I defensive? If so, why? What was I defending?
- Am I accepting the facts of the situation exactly as they are?

- Who am I being in this situation? A victim? Myself?

- What do I really want in this relationship?

- How do I want to feel?

- How does this person want to feel?

- Am I willing to move forward, to apologize where appropriate, to make an effort to understand, to offer good intentions regardless of their response?

- Am I choosing to spend my energy and my time feeling offended, when I could let this go and move on?

Often there are family members who have no idea how their remarks affect others. The mother who sends weight loss information to her overweight daughter doesn't get it that her overtures are hurtful, not helpful. The best way to help her daughter is to love her and accept her as she is. If the daughter is to release the hurt feelings and irritation she must stop blaming the mother. Often we desire family members to make improvements or take better care of themselves. We have to ask ourselves if the desire is for them, or is it for ourselves. When we deeply care about another's welfare, our encouragement may be accepted. When our intention is really about our own convenience or embarrassment, we will meet resistance. It is important to remember that people in our families are persons to be cared for, not objects to be fixed or changed.

Many of our family issues come from boundaries that are not clear. If you don't want advice or interference, tell the family member you don't want it. Be compassionate and direct. It is not your problem if they don't like it. If you are meddling in another's affairs, withdraw. Offer your respect and support.

We must realize that the remarks and actions of family members often hurt because there is already hurt within us. As we let go of our own guilt and self-blaming, the remarks of others have less meaning. In his book, *10 Secrets for Success and Inner Peace*, Dr. Wayne Dyer writes: "There are no justified resentments." Resentments become reasons for returning to our old ways. It is our inner peace that is affected when we hold on to resentments. In the same book Dr. Dyer writes, "Stop looking for occasions to be offended." As we learn to become a person who refuses to be offended by anyone we gain control over our thoughts and emotions.

Family situations often challenge us to give up blaming. Consider taking the challenge. Free yourself from the need to judge other members and from the idea that you must meet their approval. Be you, and compassionately allow others to be who they are. Speak your truth when necessary and create clear boundaries. The only thing that stands between you and your freedom is you.

If family issues are weighing you down, get help. Free yourself of the past and live powerfully in this present moment. Detach from the idea that others should change and focus your energy on being you. A professional therapist can help you to establish and maintain clear boundaries for yourself. This you do out of self-love and love for others. Your ability to be yourself is the greatest gift you can give your family, whether or not they appreciate it.

Summary: Blaming family members weighs us down. Let go of blame and you are free. Release your need for your family to be any different than what it is. Love and accept them as they are. As you move beyond blaming your level of present-day involvement is up to you. In other words, you are guided by your own Inner Voice, not the approval or disapproval of others.

19 The Addiction to Blaming: Breaking Free

The most difficult challenge in moving beyond blaming is overcoming our addiction to it. Addiction to blaming is not a metaphor; it is a psychological and physiological fact. It begins in your brain.

Your brain is made up of billions of tiny nerve cells called neurons. Neurons connect to other neurons. These connections form networks called neuronets. Each neuronet contains information—thoughts, skills, memories, beliefs, assumptions, and knowledge. All of these bits of information are represented by neuronets. Each time you learn something new your brain creates a new neuronet. If you do something once you will create a loose connection. When you repeat something over and over again, when you practice a reaction or behavior, a new neuronet is created. This is called learning.

The brain is continually adding new neuronets as we learn and grow. As the learning that is represented in a neuronet is repeated, the pathway between the neurons is strengthened. When we practice a physical or a mental skill and become proficient, we can do it easily without having to think about it. Just as we learn knowledge and skills, we learn to blame.

By constantly repeating my blaming thoughts I establish neuronets in my brain related to the blaming situation. Repetitive negative reactions become hard-wired into the brain through constant repetition and practice. Whether you are blaming your spouse, your boss, or your kids, each time you practice the blaming reaction you reinforce the neuronets. After a time you don't have to think about it. A certain look, a distinct tone of voice, or the appearance of familiar circumstances serve as stimuli, and your brain and body respond. Each time you blame these people or situations you think the same thoughts, make the same assumptions, and draw the same conclusions. It becomes subconscious. Blaming becomes automatic.

Blaming is usually emotional. When we blame, our bodies react. Chemicals, called peptides, are produced in the hypothalamus of the brain whenever we experience emotion. Cells in the brain and body have receptor sites that serve as a docking point to allow the chemicals to enter the cells. Receptor sites are molecules on the surface of a cell. When the chemicals enter the cells through the receptor sites we feel something. Dr. Candace Pert, who was one of the first to find receptor sites, termed these peptides and receptor sites "molecules of emotion".

It was found that every emotion had a brain chemical (neuropeptide) and corresponding receptor sites on cells in the body. It is the absorption of the chemical by these cells that creates the "feeling" of a specific emotion. Repetitive overuse of the chemicals creates a state of addiction.

In addiction, certain cells are being bombarded at high intensity. The cell becomes dependent on the chemical. The chemical could be an external drug such as an opiate, or it could be the chemical of anger or stress. Over time cells become desensitized so that the same amount of a chemical creates a smaller response. The cell needs more of the chemical. Each time you blame and feel it emotionally, you are feeding your cells the substance they have come to need. In other words, you become addicted to the feeling of the negative emotion. You become addicted to being the victim. You become addicted to feeling self-righteous. You come to need the negative feelings you experience. You become addicted to being angry at your spouse, or to feeling bullied by your boss, or feeling lonely and abandoned. You may not like the feeling, but you need it.

If you are creating a negative emotional state and you are unable to control it, you are addicted to it. It runs you. This is why people tend to create the same negative situations again and again. In relationships some people are addicted to being abandoned. They fantasize about being left; they strive to hold onto a relationship to prevent being left; and eventually they are left. A woman in this state may say something like: "Men always leave." The truth is that all men don't leave, just the ones she chooses. She is constantly creating and recreating the scenario of being left. She may blame men, or blame her parents, but it is she who creates the situation. She is addicted to the negative emotions that arise when she thinks about being left.

Others are addicted to being wronged. A friend of mine constantly tells stories of being treated unfairly. When she tells the story it is as if she is reliving it in front of me. All the stories are the same. Someone does something to wrong her. She becomes indignant and tells them what she thinks. There is a satisfaction gained in being the one who is right. There is an emotional and chemical charge that comes from this repetitive story. She is addicted to being the victim and being right about it.

This is why it can be difficult to move beyond blaming. You may decide you want to change, to take responsibility, but then your physiology gets in the way. Your cells want to be fed the chemicals they have come to depend upon. You seem unable to control it. That's why it is called addiction. The good news is that your brain and body are designed to learn and evolve. You can create new neuronets. You can change your reactions and create new responses to situations. You can redesign your cells.

It begins with the intention to create something different. At one point I found myself blaming my spouse quite often. I recognized that this was more my problem than it was hers. I decided I wanted a change. I didn't go to her and tell her I needed her to change. I knew that I needed to change. I began with my intention to change, to be more accepting of her and more in control of my reactions. I began observing myself. My chemical high was about feeling wronged and feeling that I was the "good one" in the relationship. I was continually recreating scenes where I could experience this reaction. Although it felt unpleasant, and I told myself I needed her to change, the truth was I needed for her to "wrong" me. Each time I felt wronged, my cells received the brain chemicals they needed. You could say that the reason I became angry with my wife was to feed my cells. We are not talking about the occasional anger you may feel toward someone. We are talking about repetitive negative emotions that seem out of our control. Getting angry doesn't mean you are addicted. Getting angry often and being unable to control the feeling is addiction.

My next step was to observe my emotional reaction, but to decide not to go there. I stopped feeding the feeling with repetitive negative thoughts. I stopped blaming. I took ownership of my negative emotions. At the same time, I started being more responsive to my wife. That is, I began paying more attention to her feelings and being concerned for her. This created a new feeling in me. I liked caring about her and being concerned for her. I began to see how I had moved away from that and become more self-centered over the past few years. I had justified my behavior by blaming her. I began seeing her emotions as her expression of her needs, rather than as something threatening to me. I began paying more attention to her many good qualities and to the reasons why I love her. It didn't happen overnight, but over a few months I let go of my addiction to blaming.

The net result for me in this process was that the intensity of my negative emotion greatly diminished. I still blame at times, but I don't take it too seriously. I may get upset and express my feelings, but then I let it go. Some days it is more difficult than others. For example, if I am already feeling badly about other things, it is easy to blame and become upset. The greatest benefit I have realized is that I feel more love and appreciation, more concern, and more joy being together. It is always more pleasing to love and appreciate than it is to blame and feel bad.

When you begin this process your cells may not be happy about it. They are crying out for the chemical produced by your negative emotions. Your cells will decay. However, new cells will be created in their place. Eventually new cells will reflect your new patterns and will not be addicted. In your brain, the neuronets you had created for blaming will begin to recede from lack of use. New neuronets will be created by the new responses you are learning.

This is a constant change process. Whenever you find yourself in the throes of negative emotion that repeats itself, you have work to do. Here are the steps as I have practiced them:

1. Notice that you have a repetitive negative emotion that you are not controlling.

2. Create the intention to make a change.

3. Observe yourself reacting. Don't judge yourself for it.

4. Own the emotions. That is, stop blaming someone else for how you feel and acknowledge that you are the maker of your emotion.

5. Make a decision not to go there and to release the emotion. You may ask yourself: "Am I willing to let this go?"

6. Become more responsive to people around you. Recognize that you need not take their emotions personally. Be concerned for them.

7. Decide how you want to feel instead (strong, powerful, compassionate, etc.). Create thoughts that bring out these new positive emotions.

Keep practicing. Don't give up. You may fail many times, but your intention and willingness to feel better will get you through.

Don't forget to acknowledge your successes. Breathe and recognize that you are not your negative emotion. You have emotions. You experience emotions. But you are not your emotion. You need not identify yourself with your emotions. You are the experiencer and the observer of your thoughts and emotions. This way of thinking will offer you greater power and control over your emotions. It frees you from all of the negative meaning you have given to your emotional reactions. Emotions are just your body's response to your thoughts. Feel them. Let them go. Experience them. Let them go. Practice letting go often and you will become adept at it.

There are many techniques available that assist people in releasing negative emotion. You will find some of these referenced in the bibliography of this book.

People all over the world behave insanely, killing each other, destroying property, offending and being offended by each other. These out-of-control emotions are addictions. People are feeding their cells when they feel self-righteous indignation toward the other side. Their hurt, their need for revenge, and their desire to strike out control them. If you find yourself in an insane situation where people are blaming and attacking each other, you have to get control of your emotions before you can help to remedy the situation. You have to stop blaming the other side for the way you feel. When we, as individuals, become more willing and able to own our negative emotions we will begin to see more harmony in our world.

Summary: Repetitive blaming becomes hard-wired into our brains and the very cells of our bodies. We become addicted to the emotions of blaming. We can overcome our addiction with our intention and willingness to let it go. You are not your emotions. You experience emotions. As the observer of your thoughts and emotions, you are capable of releasing them and creating positive emotion instead.

20 The Spirit of Blamelessness

Moving beyond blaming is made difficult by deeply ingrained thinking patterns and the emotions that accompany them. It only takes a moment to become completely immersed in hurt, anger, and anxiety. You are aware of your feelings. You find yourself of two minds — one that wants to be angry, to strike out at the other person or to be recognized as the victim. On another level of thinking you may want to release these feelings and feel emotional calm. In this mind you know that you are not a victim, or at least that blaming isn't going to make you any happier. You may feel trapped in your emotion, at least for the moment.

In these times you can appreciate your ability to be aware of yourself. This is not a time to blame yourself. This is a time to appreciate your ability to be aware and to take care of your emotions. Take care of your emotions by just feeling them. If possible, find time and space to be alone and feel the emotion without thinking about it. Be in this present moment. You will find that if you just feel the emotion without resisting it, without trying to make it go away, it will pass on its own.

This is a time where your spirituality will help you to release blaming emotions. For some, total acceptance of one's emotion is a spiritual act. You sit still and become peaceful. You see yourself as connected to all of life. Your emotions are like a passing storm. You may feel like you are on a boat being tossed about by this storm. As you accept this emotion, you become more than the boat. You become the ocean, the clouds, the storm itself. You encompass all. However you choose to envision your emotions, one thing is clear. You are not your emotions.

You are not your body. You are not your blaming thoughts. These are things you experience.

If you are not your body or your thoughts, then what are you? You are the observer and the experiencer, the witness. This is the deeper you. Spirituality is about identifying with this deeper you rather than identifying with your personality. The personality will always experience ups and downs. You are not your personality. You have a personality. You are the observer, the Thinker behind your personality. Through the practice of becoming the observer you will increase your ability to calm yourself. You will find that you can step back and observe the emotions and behaviors of self and others. The "you" that is observing all this is unharmed by it. This is not saying you should stand back and act as if you don't care. You should care deeply, but observe without judging. Observe without blaming.

In order to move beyond blaming a spiritual context can be helpful. This provides you with the strength to resolve inner conflict and heal negative emotions. Your ability to move beyond blaming can be greatly increased through spiritual practice. Spiritual practice may include prayer, meditation, contemplation, or some kind of meditative movement (Yoga, Tai Chi, some types of martial arts, walking, running, breathing exercises).

Meditation and prayer offer opportunity to move beyond negativity and blaming. I would like to summarize a three part meditation I learned from a booklet entitled: *The Song of Prayer*, by the Foundation for Inner Peace. This is my summary:

Part One—The Gift—You offer up your problem, your negative emotions, your desirable outcomes and any stress and strain you feel to God, or Oneness. You give it all away and let it go. In giving it away as a gift it is no longer yours to worry about.

Part Two—The Song—You join with God or Oneness in It's Song of Love. Focus your thinking on being completely loved and accepted by God or Oneness. Offer your gratitude for this Love. See this Love, this spiritual action, as being active in every part of your life. Trust that all is well. Don't worry about outcomes. Focus only on joining with God or Oneness.

Part Three—The Echo—This is what happens as a result of your shift in perception. You don't make this happen; Spirit does. You allow the Echo of the Song by letting go and trusting. The Echo is often the solution, the idea, or the opportunity you need to resolve a situation.

This process must be done repetitively because it is our tendency to worry and try to make it happen. Your only job is to do what is before you to do, and pay attention to the Inner Voice as inspiring ideas will come to you. You will need to act on the ideas.

Spirituality is different than religion. Religion is often a source of blaming. Religion often divides the saved from the damned, those who know from those who don't know, and the good from the evil. A religious context can be judgmental. However, every religion has an underlying spiritual tradition. While religion often divides, spirituality unites. It does not make distinctions between levels of rightness or goodness. Spirituality is about your relationship to a Higher Power, to All Power, or to the Source of All Good. Spirituality always recognizes the oneness of all life. Spirituality is acceptance. Many people who are not affiliated with formal religion are very spiritual.

This is not to say religion has no value. There is certainly value in like-minded people gathering together to learn and to support one another, practice meaningful rituals, and honor God or Oneness. Religion can teach us helpful spiritual practices. It can provide guidelines for healthy and happy living.

There are aspects of religion that keep us in the blaming mode. Guilt, condemnation, and self-righteousness based on religious arrogance can be very destructive. Blaming based on religion has caused wars and other acts of violence, the destruction of cultures, and hatred between religions, ethnic groups, families, and individuals. Religious blaming has people doing and saying things that completely violate the spiritual tradition of the religion.

In the past few years "religious" people have beaten and killed gay people; shot and killed doctors who performed abortions; killed, robbed, and raped people because they were Muslims; committed terrorist acts killing thousands of people in the name of God; and justified all sorts of violent and self-serving acts. Historically, people have always used religion to justify blaming and acting on that blame.

True spirituality is not about doctrines, who is right, or who is wrong. It is not about condemning people to hell or saying they have bad karma. Spirituality is a safe place within where peace can be found. It is a place where you find unity with God or Oneness, and total acceptance. It's not about whether you pray correctly or meditate in the right way. Spirituality is about approaching God, or Oneness with the intention to be changed (in your mind), to receive answers, and to have no preconceived notions about the answers you will find. Spirituality is total openness to Divine Guidance. In a sense, it requires you to forget what you think you already know and to humbly open yourself to thinking differently.

If you have a spiritual path or if you have certain spiritual practices, use what you have to help you move beyond blaming. Use it to find the strength you need to make good decisions. Use it to manage tumultuous emotions and the tendency to blame self and others. Don't pray that others change their ways; pray that you can change your way of seeing them. Pray that you would have the strength and the wisdom to stop judging and see truly. Your ability to see more clearly is powerful.

In Chapter Eight, we talked about self-deception and self-betrayal. Self-betrayal is when we ignore the intuitive feeling within to respond to a person or situation. We feel a strong inclination to take an action and we choose not to respond. For me, this intuitive feeling is part of my spirituality. I operate on a continuous request for guidance, and my intuitive feelings are the means through which I receive it. This is the Inner Voice. This is not the same as the critical voice in the mind. The critical voice is your ego attempting to keep you under control. The Inner Voice seeks to free you and guide you. Accessing this quality that is within each of us takes an intention to do so, and practice. Practice helps you to distinguish between your Inner Voice, and ideas that are ego-based. Your Inner Voice helps you to make decisions that are highest and best for all concerned.

Deeply spiritual people know that the source of what they need or desire is spiritual. This helps them to take their attention away from specific people and things as providers of sustenance. It causes them to know that blaming people and situations is based on the mistake that they somehow are the source of what we need. The focus is to seek first the "Kingdom of Heaven," which lies not in some far-off galaxy, but within us. As we seek this place, all else will be added. Knowing this, you are thankful for the satisfaction of your needs before you see the physical evidence. You live under the assumption that you are blessed and supplied abundantly.

If you see yourself as spiritual, then your focus needs to shift inward for the satisfaction of your needs. With an inward focus there is nothing and no one to blame. When you blame people or situations you are making them your "god." In a spiritual context people and situations are not the source of what you need. People and situations are channels of expression. People and situations can never be everything to you. People make mistakes. Situations come and go. Your trust is placed in the Divine. With a clear focus on God, or Oneness, as your Source, blaming is an error. It is something to be processed and released in order to realign with the spiritual.

Most spiritual traditions, including both Christianity and Buddhism, teach the Universal Law of Cause and Effect. This law may be read as: "You reap what you sow." Many interpret this to mean that our bad deeds will be punished, either by eternal damnation or by holding bad karma. Having bad karma means that you will reincarnate in conditions that will repay you for your past deeds, good or bad. Actually, the Universal Law is much more immediate. "What you are living today is as a result of the thoughts and feelings that you have felt before this. Your future is created from your perspective of today." (*A New Beginning II*, by Jerry and Esther Hicks)

Our perspective on life, including our beliefs, assumptions, and perceptions, draw to us people and situations that are in agreement. "Whenever you feel negative emotion, you are in the mode of negative attraction. Most often you are in that moment, resisting something you want." (*A New Beginning II*, by Jerry and Esther Hicks). When we are able to release negative emotion and move beyond blaming; when we are able to focus our attention on the joyous and healthy circumstances that we desire; relationships and situations begin to change for the better. Blaming people and situations perpetuates the misery we feel, and often the condition itself. We receive as we believe.

True spirituality is powerful. It begins with the suspicion that you are much more than you thought you were. As you progress you find that you are more (not more than others, more than what you thought you were). As you discover that you are more your life comes to reflect that understanding.

Summary: Practice observing your thoughts, emotions, and behaviors. You are not your thoughts and emotions; you are the observer. As you practice observing you find a place of calm, a place of not feeling threatened. Find that Inner Voice within you and listen. Practice prayer, meditation, and/or contemplation. Ask for help in letting go of blame. Seek first that spiritual place within you. Align yourself with the Universal Law of Cause and Effect. Your thinking creates your life.

21 Unleashing Yourself from Blame

Blame is a short leash that holds you in place. It causes you misery and lost opportunities. As a victim you have no power. Blaming makes you unhappy. It is a focus on people or things you cannot control. It is an inability to see the present moment and the abundance of possibilities and opportunities available to you.

Your power is in this present moment. It doesn't matter what has happened to you. It doesn't matter what you have done in the past. The important questions are:

- What have you learned from your past experiences?
- Where are you now?
- Where do you want to go?
- What is your vision?
- Are you willing to give up being a victim?
- Are you willing to take complete responsibility for your life, your work, and your relationships?
- Are you willing to manage your thoughts, to not let them run away in negative fantasies, suspicions, and blaming?

- Are you willing to respond to others? Will you allow yourself to be concerned for their needs?

- Will you listen to the Inner Voice and follow it?

You are equipped for greatness. There is nothing stopping you except your thoughts. There are physical realities you must accept. How you see them determines your ability to succeed. If you tell yourself that you must have a certain person or situation to be okay, you are setting yourself up for blaming and being a victim. Envision what you want, and be open to it coming from any direction.

Moving beyond blaming isn't easy. If it were easy, everyone would be doing it. It is worth it. It is not something you accomplish and then you are done. It is an ongoing process of learning and discipline. It is a continuous consciousness that you are the common denominator. You are the one who is creating your emotions. You are constantly susceptible to the urge to blame. You will always find yourself wanting to blame. Your intention to move beyond blame and into your power will constantly remind you to let go of the blaming.

Without blame you are 100% responsible. You are able to respond to any person and any situation. Blaming encourages inaction or reaction. Power inspires effective action. As a powerful person you know that your needs are met from within you. You don't have to seek it from others. You don't have to be needy or overly aggressive. You don't have to get anyone to do anything. Your presence and your way of being can inspire and influence others. A person who offers service without need for praise, often gets praised. A person who is responsive to others without need for attention to self, usually gets plenty of attention.

The idea here is that blaming is a focus on externals. We think that good things come to us from the outside and that we have to somehow get them. We think we have to hunt for it, conquer it, or beg for it. When we are clear about what we want, powerful, and responsive to others, we draw what we want to us. Here are a few examples:

A beautiful, confident woman walks into the room. All of the men except one are staring at her. The one man notices her, but he doesn't stare. He notices that all the others are staring. It's likely she will find him the most interesting man in the room, because he doesn't need for her to notice him.

Sales people who need for their customers to buy are less successful. Sales people whose focus is on their customers' needs are usually more successful.

The manager who gives credit to his people for a job well done rather than taking credit for himself, wins the loyalty of his people. People give him credit anyway.

The speaker who tries to manipulate his audience is less successful than the speaker who knows how to be himself in front of a group.

The teacher who is more concerned about her students' learning than she is about her teaching, will find greater success.

The author, artist, musician, entrepreneur, or creative person who has vision and focuses on expressing her gifts will eventually find success. The creative person who worries about why people aren't noticing or buying, who is angered at a perceived lack of success, who blames people and events for her seeming failure, is less likely to find success.

Focus on what is within you. Envision what you want and make the assumption that you can succeed. This will unleash your passion. Focus your passion on your goal, your vision. Focus your thoughts on what you can do. Focus on the best outcome. You don't have to wait for things to change to feel good about yourself. A focus on externals has us believing that goal attainment will make us feel good. It may, but why wait? Teach yourself to feel good now. Your feeling good will help you to attain your goal.

The attainment of a goal is not what makes you successful. Success is a gift you give yourself. You create your goal. You make your plans. You refuse to attach your well-being to the outcome. You tell yourself that you are okay right now. You offer yourself unconditional positive regard right now. This is a success mindset.

Over the years I have met several people who lost weight with Weight Watchers. Not only had their body changed, their personalities changed. One woman I knew was loud and often rude toward others. She became more quiet, warm toward others, and confident. I found that she was able to lose the weight after she learned to increase her appreciation for herself and others. She changed who she was being and found appreciation within herself. She no longer needed to engage in excessive eating and attention-getting behaviors.

We live our lives from the inside out. We create our own experience. There is no blame. There is no self-blame. You are where you are. You can respond or not. Each of us has the power and the passion to live fulfilling lives. Together we can build successful organizations, families, and relationships. You can choose to envision the possibilities and respond to people, or you can blame. It is a decision you make. What kind of relationship do you want? What kind of organization do you want for your work? What kind of family do you want? What kind of life do you want? Your joy and success in all aspects of life are waiting for you.

It all comes down to your thinking. Where do you focus your thoughts? Where is your emotional energy flowing? You are giving to life that which is inside of you. If you truly want to unleash your power and passion, you need to manage your thoughts.

Try this: Get yourself a notebook and call it "My Positive Features Book". (Note: This is adapted from an idea given in *A New Beginning II*, by Jerry and Esther Hicks.) Sit down and list everything in your life that is positive. Scan your work, your relationships, your finances, your health, your family, your home, your activities, your gifts and talents, events that occurred today, and write down every positive thing you see, feel, or have. If you have $500 in the bank, write that down. If you find yourself saying that $500 isn't enough, stop that thought. The purpose of this exercise is to focus on what you do have, not on what you don't. Focus on what you have. Read what you have written. Tomorrow, read your list and write another list. Do this every day and you will begin to feel better. As you feel better you will see things differently. You will draw to you more positive conditions.

Do this same thing with any difficult people in your life. Write down everything you can appreciate about them. Do this every day until you feel differently toward them. You will feel better toward them after a time if that is your intent. You will find this person responding to you in a more positive way. Your power is found in how you see yourself and others. Your opinion of self or others is your vision. Just as my first manager, Ted, held a vision that uplifted me, your ability to view the good in others will serve to uplift them—and you. I have done this exercise with myself regarding people I did not like. I found myself changing my view and my way of relating to them. I gave them someone different to respond to and they responded differently to me.

Most people are not very picky about the thoughts they allow into their minds. Powerful people are picky about their choice of thoughts. They choose to think well of others. They may not think well of someone's behavior, but they will think well of the person. Your willingness and ability to think well of someone is a key factor in helping them to change their negative behavior. Is this guaranteed? Of course it isn't. Having power doesn't mean you can solve everything. Do your best. You can't help but feel negative emotion, but you don't have to hang onto it.

Move your thinking toward what you really want. Focus your thoughts and energy on the success you would create and on the good that is already created. As you cultivate thoughts that make you feel good, you uplift yourself. You find yourself attracting more of what you truly want. Refuse to allow anyone or anything to talk you out of feeling good. As you shift your thinking toward more thoughts that make you feel good, you will find more people who want to feel good wanting to be around you.

There is immense power in learning how to feel good. We are not talking about the feeling good that comes from substances like alcohol, drugs, cigarettes, or any number of things that people tend to use in addictions. Feeling good can be created at any moment by your intention. You simply focus on the good feelings you want to have.

When I am feeling down I allow myself to feel down for a time. When I am ready to move on, I ask myself if I am willing to release the negative feelings. Next, I think thoughts of gratitude for all of my blessings. I think about visions I want to create and feel the good feelings that come with them. When I find myself complaining I remind myself that I don't want to go there. I step back and look at my assumptions, and focus my energy on what I want to create. I am not perfect at these mind shifts. Through practice I have learned to manage my mind and my emotions with greater skill. This is a blessing to me and to everyone around me.

As you become more blameless you start to feel different on the inside. You are less likely to get upset with others. You are less likely to be upset with yourself. You spend more time feeling good. Your relationships change in a significant way. There is a significant drop in the amount of stress and conflict you feel with others. You are much more at peace. As you let go of your need to influence others, you feel more at peace. Your influence begins to grow. You feel more powerful. You find more joy and passion in all that you do.

You know that you create your own experience by way of your thoughts and emotions. Every day life will throw people and opportunities in your direction. It's your call. Is it good or not good? Does it have any effect on your well-being? It's your call. Your power and passion are ready to be unleashed. You can find it all within you in a place that is beyond blaming.

Summary: Practice thinking good thoughts. Withdraw your need for specific others to give you what you want. Blamelessness will bring you peace. It will lift up your life. Your power and passion will be unleashed.

Bibliography: Quoted Books and Other Helpful Readings and Influences

Arbinger Institute	*Leadership and Self-Deception*, Berret-Koehler Publishers, 2002 *The Choice*, Arbinger Institute, 1998 www.arbinger.com
Artz, William Chasse, Betsy Vicente, Mark	*What the Bleep Do We Know? Discovering the Endless Possibilities For Altering Your Everyday Reality*, Health Communications, 2005
Aung Sang Suu Kyi	*The Voice of Hope*, Seven Stories Press, 1997
Carlson, Richard Bailey, Joseph	*Slowing Down to The Speed of Life*, HarperSanFrancisco, 1997
Covey, Stephen R.	*The 7 Habits of Highly Effective People*, Simon and Schuster, 1989
Deming, W. Edwards	*Out of The Crisis*, M.I.T., 1982

Dwoskin, Hale	*The Sedona Method: Your Key to Lasting Happiness, Success, and Emotional Well-being,* Sedona Press, 2003
Dyer, Dr. Wayne	*10 Secrets for Success and Inner Peace,* Hay House, Inc., 2001
Fisher, Roger Ury, William	*Getting To Yes,* Penguin Books, 1981
Foundation for Inner Peace	*The Song of Prayer,* Foundation for Inner Peace, 1978
Frankl, Dr. Victor;	*Man's Search for Meaning,* Simon and Schuster, 1970
Goleman, Daniel	*Emotional Intelligence,* Bantam Books, 1995
Hawkins, Dr. David	*Power Vs. Force,* Hay House, Inc., 1995
Hicks, Jerry and Esther	*A New Beginning II,* Abraham-Hicks Publications, 1991
McGraw, Dr. Phillip	*Life Strategies,* Hyperion Books, 1999
Pert, Dr. Candace	*Molecules of Emotion,* Scribner, 1997
Senge, Peter	*The Fifth Discipline,* Currency Doubleday, 1990

Tolle, Eckhardt — *Practicing the Power of Now*, New World Library, 2001

Zander, Rosamund Stone
Zander, Benjamin — *The Art of Possibility*, Penguin Books, 2002

Leadership: An Art of Possibility (Video)

The following Web sites contain information about alternative healers and therapies for dealing with emotions and emotional blockages.

www.nlpinfo.com
www.emofree.com
www.aetw.com

Information on emotional release techniques can be found by reading the book, *The Sedona Method* or by visiting: www.sedona.com.

Visit www.emofree.com to learn about Gary Craig's emotional release techniques. Download his free manual, whichteaches you how to use the Emotional Freedom Technique.

Learn about Neuro Linguistic programming at www.nlpinfo.com.

Learn about various types of energy healing at: www.aetw.com.

Acknowledgments

I would like to thank friends and colleagues who read this book and gave me valuable feedback. I am grateful to Jon Nelson, Rob Curtner, Mary Lawton, Peter Dougherty, and my wife, Peggy Diedrich. Thank you to Sharon Berman for her excellent editing. I am grateful to everyone in my life who I have blamed for anything. To all of you, I say thank you for teaching me.

I am grateful for spiritual guidance in the forms of intuition and inspiration. I don't always have to know what to say or what to write, because if I listen, it will come to me. Thank you to my son, Joshua Diedrich for his design work on this book. Special thanks to Lyle Swinehart for lending us a hand. Lastly, thank you to all of my teachers, including those listed on my Bibliography page.

I am grateful to the great spiritual teachers who are quoted in this book, including Jesus the Christ and the Buddha. Modern spiritual teachers who I have quoted or whose example is mentioned include Mahatma Gandhi, Martin Luther King Jr. and Aung Sang Suu Kyi.